YEAR OF THE
RIPPERS

THE DR. WILLIAM SCARLET MYSTERIES

Red Season

YEAR OF THE RIPPERS

GARY GENARD

Cedar &
Maitland
Press

First Edition

Cover design: Llywellyn.

Interior typesetting: Lorna Reid

Illustration: Lydia Genard

ISBN: 978-1-7365556-6-8

Library of Congress Control Number: 2024905746

Printed in the United States of America

To order this book, please call (617) 993-3410, or contact info@garygenard.com. Group discounts are available.

Visit the author's website at www.garygenard.com. Join our mailing list!

To Mary Ann Nichols, Annie Chapman,
Elizabeth Stride, Catherine Eddowes, and
Mary Jane Kelly

Now Atropos, one of the three Fates—
The Inflexible One, who with her scissors
Severs the vital thread of life—
Has grown big with blood,
And it is our right (for we are Furies)
To avenge her victims when the blessings
Of the gods were not granted to her.

Aeschylus, *The Eumenides* [fragment from an early draft]

*

Men feel that they are face to face with some awful and extraordinary freak of nature. So inexplicable and ghastly are the circumstances surrounding the crimes that the mind turns instinctively to some theory of occult force and the myths of the Dark Ages . . . ghouls, vampires, bloodsuckers and all the ghastly array of fables which have been accumulated throughout the course of centuries take form, and seize hold of the excited fancy. Yet the most morbid imagination can conceive nothing worse than this terrible reality; for what can be more appalling than the thought that there is a being in human shape stealthily moving about a great city, burning with the thirst for human blood, and endowed with such diabolical astuteness as to enable him to gratify his fiendish lust with absolute impunity.

East London Advertiser, 6 October 1888

PROLOGUE

The Second Murder

DIVISIONAL REFERENCE H302

Submitted through Ex: Bch: H Division

Commercial Street 300/1
METROPOLITAN POLICE.
H Division.
8th September 1888

I beg to report that at 6.10 a.m. 8th inst. while on duty in Commercial Street, Spitalfields, I received information that a woman had been murdered. I at once proceeded to No. 29 Hanbury Street, and in the back yard found a woman lying on her back, dead, left arm resting on left breast, legs drawn up, abducted small intestines and flap of the abdomen lying on right side, above right shoulder attached by a cord with the rest of the intestines inside the body; two flap of skin from the lower part of the abdomen lying in a large quantity of blood above the left shoulder; throat cut deeply from left and back in a jagged manner right around throat. I at once sent for Dr. Phillips Div. Surgeon and to the Station for the ambulance and assistance. The Doctor pronounced life extinct and stated the woman had been dead at least two hours. The body was then removed on the Police ambulance to the Whitechapel mortuary.

On examining the yard I found on the back wall of the house (at the head of the body) and about 18 inches from the ground about 6 patches of blood varying in size from a sixpenny piece to a point, and on the wooden pailing on left of the body near the head patches and smears of blood about 14 inches from the ground.

The woman has been identified by Timothy Donovan "Deputy" Crossinghams Lodging house 35 Dorset Street, Spitalfields, who states he has known her about 16 months, as a prostitute and for the past 4 months she had lodged at above house and at 1.45 a.m. 8th inst. she was in the kitchen, the worse for liquor and eating potatoes, he Donovan sent to her for the money for her bed, which she said she had not got and asked him to trust her which he declined to do she then left stating that she would not be long gone; he saw no man in her company.

Description, Annie Siffey age 45, length 5 ft, complexion fair, hair (wavy) dark brown, eyes blue, two teeth deficient in lower jaw, large thick nose; dress black figured jacket, brown bodice, black skirt, lace boots, all old and dirty.

A description of the woman has been circulated by wire to All Stations and a special enquiry called for at Lodging Houses &c to ascertain if any men of a suspicious character or having blood on their clothing entered after 2 am 8th inst.

JL.Chandler Inspr.

nnie Chapman—sometimes known as "Siffey," "Sivvey," or "Sievey" because she had lived with a man who was a sieve maker—was found murdered two days after the funeral of Mary Ann Nichols, slain eight days earlier. The awful possibility that a crazed killer was stalking London's East End seemed to have been confirmed.

Three more murders like this one would follow over the next three months, before the toll of women slaughtered and mutilated by a shadowy killer finally ended in November. Or so it seemed. In reality, there would be *seven* more killings—though the world would never connect four of them with the soon-to-become famous murderer of London prostitutes in Whitechapel and Spitalfields.

Most curious of all, the monster known as "Jack the Ripper" would have nothing to do with any of these killings.

The narrative that follows concerns what actually happened in London in the summer and fall of The Year of Our Lord eighteen hundred and eighty-eight. It is the true story of that awful time, told at last.

CHAPTER 1

Doss Houses and Phossy Jaw

hitechapel is a section of London's East End, though to its residents in the year 1888 it may have seemed more like the world's end. It was a place of desperate poverty and a constant struggle to survive.

To the fur pullers who cleaned rabbit skins for a living and worked in enclosed places filled with fluff and hair, it was a struggle just to breathe. To the masses who overburdened the labor market in the area, it was a never-ending struggle to find work. To the girls who worked in the match factories, it was a doomed effort to avoid "phossy jaw," in which the phosphorous from the matches ate away their jaws and then killed them. To the fallen women forced to walk the streets for immoral purposes after midnight, lifting their skirts while braced against a grimy brick wall—London's "unfortunates"—it was a struggle to gain the few pence necessary to secure a bed for the night.

The doss houses, or common lodging places, were waiting for them when they succeeded.

A doss house would provide you with a bed in an overcrowded dormitory for four pence a night, and where you could use the central kitchen to cook whatever you were able to scrounge or steal that day. For low-wage working men, prostitutes, and anyone desperately down on their luck, it offered a place to spend the night that was one step up from the street.

In Whitechapel alone in the year of our story, out of a population of about a quarter million, the Metropolitan Police estimated that there were 1,200 prostitutes, and over 60 brothels. There were 149 registered doss houses or "hostels," and an unknown number of unregistered ones.

In the docks area of St George in the East, the poverty rate was nearly 49 percent. And the mortality rate in the poor quarters of England's cities was such that one of every five children didn't make it past their first year.

It was in this world of misery and desperation—where lived the People of the Abyss—that the murders began.

CHAPTER 2

"See What a Jolly Bonnet I've Got Now"

ary Ann Nichols didn't want to argue with the deputy-keeper at Wilmott's, a women-only lodging house at 18 Thrawl Street, Spitalfields, even though he was turning her away because she didn't have the money for a bed. She knew he was only doing his job. And she'd been through this little drama many times. All the same, she needed a place to sleep. Thursday, the 30th of August, 1888, had just become Friday, the 31st, and at this late hour any remaining beds would be going fast.

All the same, Mary Ann (known to her friends as "Polly") wasn't terribly concerned. For one thing, it should be easy to get the necessary funds on a warm night like this. Lifting your skirt—or for your customer, unbuttoning his trousers—could even be a relief in the hot summer night. Mary Ann was also feeling good from drink. Not drunk, mind you, but, well, *light-hearted.*

So, she laughed.

"I'll soon get my doss money," she told the lodging house deputy who was turning her away, a man named Harrington. And she added, in support of her statement: "See what a jolly bonnet I've got now!"

She was indeed wearing a bonnet she hadn't been seen with before, though "jolly" probably wasn't the best description of it. It was a straw bonnet trimmed with black velvet; but the straw was broken in places, the velvet was worn shiny, and two rows of black beads that had once adorned the hat were now missing completely.

It was after 1.00 a.m. when Mary Ann/Polly left the lodging house on Thrawl Street to seek, if not her fortune, then the 4d. she needed to rent a bed for the night. Around 2.30, her friend Ellen Holland met Polly on the corner of Whitechapel Road and Osborn Street, where the two women chatted for a few minutes. Polly was by now very drunk. As the clock at St Mary's across the road struck the half-hour, Mrs. Holland tried to convince her friend to come home with her. But Polly was determined to raise her doss money.

"I have had my lodging money three times today," she said proudly, "and I have spent it. It won't be long before I'll be back." The two women parted company. It was the last reported sighting of Polly Nichols alive.

By 3.30 a.m., when Charles Cross left his home in Bethnal Green to walk to his job as a carman for the great haulage company Pickford's, the morning was still dark, and there was a chill in the air. At around 3.40 or 3.45, Cross was walking along Buck's Row, which was located a mile and a half to the south and slightly westward from Bethnal Green. Buck's Row was a narrow street featuring very poor brick houses attached to each other in the "row" which gave the area its name. Cross noticed what he thought was a tarpaulin lying at the entrance of a stable yard on the other side of the street.

He was halfway across the street when he realized it wasn't a tarp, but the body of a woman.

He noticed another workman walking in the same direction as he was, and went up to the man and tapped him on the shoulder.

"Come and look over here," he said. "There's a woman lying on the pavement."

The other man's name was Robert Paul, and as it happened, he was also a carman. Together, the two men approached the form.

The woman was lying on her back, with her skirts raised above her waist. Cross crouched down and felt her hands. They were cold.

"I believe she's dead," he told Paul.

The other man crouched down beside Cross. To him as well, the hands and the face were cold. But when he touched the woman's chest, he thought he felt some movement.

"I think she's breathing, but very little if she is," he announced.

Both men were late in getting to work, so after a half-hearted attempt to pull the woman's skirts down, they decided they would continue on their way and alert the first policeman they might find. That was PC Jonas Mizen 55H*, who they found at the corner of Hanbury Street and Old Montague.

"She looks to me to be either dead or drunk," Cross informed the constable. "But for my part I think she is dead."

By this time, the body had been discovered separately by a policeman on his beat, PC John Neil 97J*. By the light of his lantern, Neil was able to see a deep gash in the throat, still oozing blood as the woman stared unseeingly at the night—or early morning—sky.

PC Neil was soon joined by two other policemen. He sent one of them for an ambulance and to notify Bethnal Green Police Station, and the other to fetch a doctor who lived on nearby Whitechapel Road. Dr. Rees Ralph Llewellyn was therefore on the scene shortly after four o'clock. There, he made a preliminary examination of the body.

He found that the woman's torso and legs were still warm, making him think that she hadn't been dead for more than half an hour. There was blood on the pavement, but not much; as Dr. Llewellyn described it to the press later that day: "not more than would fill two wine glasses, or half a pint at the outside." It had

---

* The letter after a police constable's number identifies the division of the Metropolitan Police Force he is stationed in. In this case, it is H division, which is the division responsible for Whitechapel.

* "J" designates the Bethnal Green Division.

probably run down into the gutter from the wound in the woman's throat.

Canvassing of houses at the scene by the policemen—including the house next to the stable yard entrance—yielded no information whatever. The residents of these houses had heard nothing unusual in the night.

Only when the victim was removed to the mortuary in Old Montague Street and her clothes lifted up was the extent of her injuries revealed.

As a police inspector summarized Dr. Llewellyn's examination: the woman had suffered two incisions in her throat, from left to right, which had cut deeply through her windpipe down to the spinal cord, severing both carotid arteries. Her right lower jaw and left cheek were bruised, as if by someone's thumb. Worst of all, her abdomen had been cut open; there was a long, deep, jagged wound through which her bowels protruded. Other incisions ran across and down her abdomen. Her vagina had been stabbed twice.

The victim was five feet two inches tall and middle-aged. Her hair was brown, though turning grey, and she was missing five front teeth. On her person were a comb, a broken mirror, and a white handkerchief. None of these facts would help much in identifying her. But it was discovered that she was wearing petticoats with "Lambeth Workhouse" written on them, and that's how she was identified. An inmate at the workhouse recognized her as Mary Ann ("Polly") Nichols—the same Mary Ann Nichols who needed to raise her doss money, she of the jolly bonnet. Nichols was a woman whose failed marriage and descent into alcoholism and prostitution represented an all-too-common tale in London's East End. The black straw bonnet had been found next to her body.

The first victim of the series of London murders of 1888 now had a name.

CHAPTER 3

A Monster in Human Shape

r. William Scarlet lowered the copy of *The Times* he was reading and looked at the man sitting across from him in an oversized leather armchair, the twin of his own. Holman Fisher (Junior) was looking at him with his eyebrows raised quizzically. Yes, Scarlet thought, that was the word for the eager manner in which young Fisher asked questions: *quizzically*. And, apparently in this case, impatiently, for he repeated himself.

"I said, are you reading about the murder of the prostitute, Mary Ann Nichols, from two days ago? I assume you didn't hear me because you were reading. Quite a shocking story for a Monday, what? Though the coverage in yesterday's Sunday edition was quite extensive as well."

"Yes, I heard you," Scarlet responded good-naturedly. "And yes, I was reading about it."

"Awful, isn't it? Do you think *The Times* is accurate?"

"Quite accurate, as far as I can tell. It pretty much dovetails with what we've given out at the Yard."

Holman Fisher's eyes widened. "Oh, what a muttonhead I am!" he proclaimed. "Of course, you're a police surgeon. I quite forgot!" He leaned forward conspiratorially, as if his next question had never been asked of a member of the Metropolitan Police.

"Is there something else you know that the public isn't aware of at this point? Can you tell me?"

Scarlet took a beat. He was tempted to remind Fisher that a woman's murder wasn't a cause for titillation—whatever her profession. But he settled for banality, which he hoped would be blasé enough to put the young man off.

"No, nothing, Junior," he said, which is what everyone in The Society called the lad. "We're pursuing every lead, and working very hard at questioning everyone in the area."

It seemed to work. Fisher nodded and shrugged at the same time, then leaned back in his chair, looking slightly crestfallen.

Scarlet could have added that Junior needn't have worried that he wouldn't hear more about the event. There was no doubt in his mind that the murder would dominate tonight's meeting of The Society for Supernatural and Psychic Research that they were both, in fact, here at Lord Nesbit's home to attend. That was the purpose of this gathering, after all—to discuss what recent occurrence The Society would adopt as its second case.[1]

The Society for Supernatural and Psychic Research was a gentlemen's club of strictly limited membership. It had a particular interest which was perfectly reflected in its name. Despite the official aura of that name, the Society was simply a group of highly successful men in their respective fields—twelve of them plus Scarlet—who shared an interest in supernatural and psychic phenomena. As such, their agenda could rest on a whim or any unusual circumstance that caught their interest—or, as Scarlet was sure would be the case tonight, a momentous event that concerned everyone in the capital. They could investigate what they wanted when they wanted to do so (using their own private funds); and any decision to publish the results of their investigations would be theirs alone.

All of the members of The Society, apart from two, understood that their role was to (A) decide on cases to pursue, (B) provide the

---

[1] See the initial book in the series, *Red Season* (Cedar & Maitland Press, 2024), for the Society's first case.

necessary resources, and (C) relish the otherworldly phenomena that a case might bring to light. Any operational duties would fall to Dr. Scarlet himself (his position as a police surgeon at Scotland Yard was invaluable in this regard), and Django Pierce-Jones, The Society's secretary and Scarlet's close friend. Pierce-Jones, who was half English and half Romani, was also a medium famous for his hand at conducting séances. He did so both privately and for the Metropolitan Police on those occasions where the Yard was stumped and asked for his help.

The group's initial meetings at their member Lord Nesbit's home in Russell Square had been so successful (and truth be told, so comfortable in terms of décor, dinner fare, and libations), that the house had become the Society's official meeting place. It was where they had gathered tonight, repairing as usual after dinner to the upper parlour. That was where Scarlet had been catching up on the day's papers before Holman Fisher (Junior) had asked his questions.

Now, the meeting came to order as John Borland, Earl of Caversham and the club's only Member of Parliament, stood and began to speak. The thirteen members of the Society were arranged all around the parlour: in armchairs, standing, or seated at the heavy boardroom table in the center of the room. The majority were sitting at the table, where the after-dinner decanters of madeira, sherry, whisky, brandy, and water were to be found. Curiously enough, the crystal cruet with water was the only container still full to the brim.

"Gentlemen," began Borland in parliamentary style. The parlour was large and, one might say, vaguely parliamentary as well in its traditional English décor. "As we consider our interest in a second case for The Society, we are struck by the timing of the recent headlines. I refer, of course, to the murder of the unfortunate two days ago in Whitechapel."

"Not in Parliament, John!" Jacob Blum, the always dour shipbuilder, chimed in. "Don't speechify."

That comment was remarkably similar to one made to the present speaker last year by Julius Pickering, founder of the

Pickering Grocers chain, when Borland had opened the Society's inaugural meeting.

Scarlet smiled to himself, wondering what he might as a medical man call this syndrome of advanced fustiness if he encountered it at St George's Hospital. *Galloping communicable contagion* might do. Or perhaps *word-dropsy*. In terminal cases, he might be forced to diagnose *irreversible Whitehall brain cementation*.

Sir Hugh Rodney, perhaps the most famous architect in England, and a man known for his incisive intelligence as well as his design skills, spoke up. From his place at the parlour's front window, he immediately cut to the chase.

"Of course, we're going to consider this murder," he said. "The disembowelment of a woman on a sidewalk in plain view, on a densely populated street? And with no one in the house next door hearing a thing? Does that sound natural?"

In a way, Sir Hugh had just expressed a view that would dominate the minds of Londoners in the coming months.

Enzo Conti, the Italian vintner and exporter, apparently having decided to play the devil's advocate, said in his genial manner: "But it was around three in the morning. No one would be awake or out walking at that time."

"On the contrary," offered another Society member, James Scorgie, the owner of *The Daily Post* newspaper, and a generally contrary person. "This was Whitechapel. Apart from the ladies of the night in that district, you have people getting up at that time to get things ready in the markets and on the docks and walking to work. There are always people around in the early hours in Whitechapel and Spitalfields."

"Hear, hear!" said Holman Fisher (Junior), he of the questions to Scarlet earlier.

But now, someone who might not have been expected to say anything, spoke up. This was Lord Nesbit, the oldest member of the club and the host of tonight's meeting. Everyone understood that, of the Society's members, he probably knew the workings of

London, from its citizens to its halls of power, better than anyone else present. He proved it now with two questions:

"Then why did the constable assigned that beat say he'd seen no one when he walked by that spot a half-hour earlier? What I mean is, aren't the policemen on these patrols always saying that they hardly ever see anyone at that hour of the morning?"

This was not an opinion but fact, as the papers had been reporting over the past two days. As facts will, it sunk in.

Lord Nesbit capped his argument by adding: "Whoever did this is a monster in human shape."

To Scarlet, gathering into camps like this made no sense. *If* they believed that Mary Ann Nichols's murder two nights ago had an otherworldly aspect, they could start their own discreet investigation, then decide whether they should continue along that course. But they certainly needed more information than was provided by two days of newspaper clippings.

There was also a more serious objection to pursuing their own inquiry: Scotland Yard. The fact was that Whitechapel—for all its reputation as a place of abject poverty and prostitution—hadn't experienced a single homicide in the previous year. People were already demanding a strong response from the Metropolitan Police to the Nichols murder, and so far the Yard was providing it. Last year, when Scarlet and Pierce-Jones had tracked down the demon in the shape of Mrs. Morana Bain, the case had been clearly within the Society's purview—and not Scotland Yard's. That the breakthrough in the case had come from a séance proved that fact.

Scarlet's own psychic ability as a psychometrist—someone who experiences visions from another person's life through touching them or an object they've handled—was a perpetual sore point with Sir Edward Mallinson, Chief Surgeon of the Metropolitan Police and Scarlet's superior. Though Sir Edward knew about Scarlet's ability with psychometry, he frowned upon him using his gift in police work. And he was adamantly opposed to one of his surgeons participating in séances or other forays into the supernatural. Scarlet and Pierce-Jones had solved last year's case precisely because there was never an official investigation begun into the events that had transpired.

This time was different. The Nichols murder was most certainly under official investigation by the Yard, so that Scarlet and the Society had no business interfering in the case. He, Scarlet, would only consider looking into it if another angle presented itself—one that the Metropolitan Police couldn't and wouldn't touch. In the two days since this woman's murder, nothing like that had shown itself. It was another reason he thought it was too early for the Society to think about looking into the murder.

These were the thoughts he was pondering when Django Pierce-Jones walked into the parlour from the hall. Scarlet welcomed the interruption. If anyone could bring a ray of sunshine into the atmosphere of an English gentlemen's club that could be as gray as its climate, it was Pierce-Jones. Of Romani heritage (his father had been a famous explorer of the Dr. Livingstone stamp who had Anglicized the family name when they emigrated to England), Django's name, in fact, meant "I awake." Scarlet had always been delighted with the combination of Django's exotic Roma background and his respectably hyphenated English last name. He had given his friend the nickname of The Roma King.

"I terribly regret being late, gentlemen," Django announced as he approached the boardroom table, looking more serious than usual. Slightly taller than Scarlet and darkly handsome, he boasted a full head of tight black curls that covered most of his ears and his collar. If you listened to Django long enough, sooner or later you would encounter one of the not-quite-right expressions that testified to his efforts to sound completely British. What he had wanted to say just now, of course, was: "Terribly sorry I'm late, gentlemen."

"We were discussing whether we should take up the case of the unfortunate who was murdered on Friday in the East End," said another Society member. That was Thaddeus ("Teddy") Locke, the tight-lipped banker.

Pierce-Jones looked confused. He said to Locke: "Unfortunate *what*, Teddy? Who is unfortunate?"

"It's a term for a woman in poverty who offers herself on the street," Scarlet enlightened him. "It's considered kinder than 'prostitute.'"

"Ah, another English euphemism," replied Django, somewhat non-committedly.

"What's your opinion?" Sir Hugh Rodney asked him. "We were discussing whether there were enough people in that neighborhood at that time of the morning to notice something. You see, if there were and no one saw or heard anything, then perhaps something unexplained occurred in the woman's murder. Something occult, perhaps. That's what we were arguing about."

Pierce-Jones nodded as he poured himself some sherry. "I would be more interested in the murder that took place tonight," he said. "It is most unexplained, as you put it, Sir Hugh." With that thunderclap, Pierce-Jones took a sip of sherry. Scarlet wondered if he was the only one who noticed that his friend's hand shook slightly.

"What?" exclaimed Joseph Trippel III, another eager young member of the club. "I've seen nothing in the papers!"

"The remains were just discovered," Pierce-Jones said in a subdued voice. "The story will be in the papers in the morning. Or, some of it will be, I imagine." He glanced at Scarlet as if to say: *"That's why you haven't heard about it yet."*

Scarlet wasn't surprised. He knew that Django had sources of his own that the Yard would only hear about belatedly, if ever. What interested him far more was his friend's use of the word 'remains,' and that cryptic last remark about 'some' of the story being in the newspapers.

All of the members were gathered around the table now where Pierce-Jones was standing. No one said, "Tell us," or "Go on, old boy." No one had to. Django, still looking terribly mysterious, took another sip of sherry.

"The body was discovered a couple of hours ago, in Green Dale

Fields, in Camberwell," he finally began. "It was found in a raised garden, and it was difficult to spot because it was getting dark. That and . . . well, it wasn't intact. The man's wallet was in the trousers, though, which was found some yards from the body. There were a few pounds in the pocket, along with a watch and chain still attached to a belt loop. So, the motive doesn't appear to have been robbery. His name was Anders Haugen, a Norwegian. I think he was a big man, someone who worked on the docks or maybe in a warehouse."

To Scarlet, the fact that Django had blurted all of this out in one go was telling. He was obviously bothered by what he was saying—traumatized might be a better word—even if Scarlet couldn't tell exactly why yet. He thought that as his friend, he should be the one to question Django more closely.

"Did you see the body?" He knew that Django's sources could have notified him early enough that he arrived at the murder site at the same time as the authorities.

"No. Yes. Close enough to get a sense of it."

What in the world was his friend talking about? Scarlet wanted to ask him point-blank what he had seen, but he didn't. Django came to it on his own.

"The poor fellow seems to have been ripped apart," he said, looking down at the tabletop. "I heard the police saying something along those lines. Anyway, I could see it from where I stood."

"You mean he was badly slashed, like the woman in Whitechapel two nights ago?" asked Scorgie, ever the newspaper owner.

"Oh, no," replied Django. "I mean exactly what I said: *he was ripped apart.* Not by a knife—no knife could do that. I could see pieces of him from where I stood, scattered around the garden." He looked straight at Scarlet. "There was blood everywhere— *everywhere.* Doesn't that mean he was still alive when it was done?"

Scarlet sat his friend down and graduated Django from sherry to brandy. Men who had fought in war—those, that is, who understood the true meaning of the term cannon fodder—might be able to encompass what Django had seen without a complete loss of equilibrium. But not any of the men in this room.

Gradually, Django got his breathing rhythm back. Next, his color returned to normal. When he looked up and spoke, his voice sounded rational.

"Shouldn't we be looking at this murder, rather than the other one?" he asked the group around the table.

The members of The Society for Supernatural and Psychic Research didn't nod just yet. But they all knew that their decision had already been made.

CHAPTER 4

Ceremony

ifteen miles from Lord Nesbit's home in Russell Square as the raven (or bat) flies, in southeast London in the borough of Bromley, lie the Chislehurst Caves. The caves are a maze of man-made tunnels, abandoned treasure chambers, and rooms whose original purposes are unknown. Also there are ancient chapels complete with altars, along with freestanding stone platforms that bear a striking resemblance to autopsy tables.

Tonight, however, it is the religious aspect of one of the carved-out chapels that is on the mind of the men gathered there to worship.

The men's appearance in robes and hoods, and the feeble glow of candles casting giant shadows on the walls are reminiscent of the Druids who excavated these caves. Or was it the Romans? Whether it was Celtic or Roman deities who were once worshipped here no longer matters, however.

On this night, the goddesses worshipped will be Greek. Not one goddess but *three,* in fact—though it is to one of these in particular that the hooded men will be offering their devotions.

She is terrible and implacable, this goddess—one who never deviates from the debt of blood she demands. But that is precisely why the men are here to worship her and ask for her help.

The celebrants of this secret rite aren't otherwise mysterious. They are in fact a cross-section of London's working-class men:

merchants, night watchmen, labourers, and dock-workers. Even a few policemen are represented, safe from discovery beneath their robes. There are twenty worshippers here tonight. When the goddess arrives, the number will be twenty-one: or seven times the pagan trinity they are paying tribute to. To such people, numbers like this mean something.

The robed men begin to hum, the otherworldly sound reverberating eerily and beautifully throughout the chamber. Now they are gathering around an altar stained with blood. No, not blood—only red paint or dye. The stain is new, and is in fact too bright and too crimson to be real blood.

This altar is curiously constructed. It is low to the ground, not more than two feet high: a stone tablet with a narrow pedestal at each end. A large circular hole has been cut in the stone directly over an opening in the ground or "denehole" that disappears into the chalky cave floor.

The reason that the altar is so low and is set above a hole in the earth is because this worship service is offered to one of the "chthonic" deities, or gods and goddesses of the underworld. The denehole is meant to receive a special kind of smoke—about to make its appearance—that flows *downwards*. It is therefore unlike ordinary smoke which rises upward toward the "ouranic" or sky-dwelling gods. For the same reason, when these worshippers kneel, they will turn the palms of their hands downward, so that their prayers can reach the deity whose dwelling place is underground.

Six objects have been placed on the red-painted stone altar, arranged around the hole in the center. They are a woman's striped stocking and a garter, a lady's comb, a used bar of soap, and three one-penny coins, dark with use. The stone of the altar itself is old and chipped, and the oil and sweat from perhaps centuries of human hands placed there has darkened the sides of the structure.

Darkness is palpable this deep underground, where noon or midnight have no meaning. It is perpetually night in this chapel . . . which is precisely why the chthonic deities come when they are called.

Now everything is silent and still. The congregants seem to be waiting for something.

From the shadows, a hooded figure appears carrying a metal cylinder. Behind him is another figure who is holding an alabaster pitcher filled with water, which he holds carefully by the handle and the bottom. The first figure goes behind the stone altar with the hole cut in the middle. The other kneels on the ground and holds a metal bowl underneath the hole.

The first figure unscrews the top of the cylinder he brought with him. Then he carefully turns the container upside-down, so that its contents fall with a clattering sound into the bowl. The kneeling one quickly pours the water from the pitcher on top of the contents. At once, smoke billows up from the bowl, like water boiling up from a swift-flowing underground stream. The smoke spills outward and downward, forming a white-grey cloud that covers the ground and flows into the denehole. It is *dry ice*, or a solid form of carbon dioxide, recently invented by a doctor in the British Army and known to the pharmacist in the robe and hood who brought it tonight.

Once the sacrificial smoke is flowing steadily into the deep hole, each congregant prostrates himself on the cave floor, his hands pressed against the cold, unforgiving rock.

One of them begins to chant a prayer.

LEADER OF WORSHIPPERS:
Goddesses of destiny, you three mighty Fates! —
You Moirai: weaving goddesses who spin, measure,
and then cut the lives of men: Clotho, Lachesis, and Atropos . . .
Hear us!
We seek justice and retribution against these wicked times,
Stroke by stroke, against those who have defiled our world.
We are the Friends of the Daughters of Night.

You, who are the children of Nyx, herself the child of Chaos
And mother to you and to her four other children:
Strife, Pain, Sleep, and Death.
Goddesses of the underworld, hear our supplications!
Of you three Fates, we summon Atropos—the Inflexible One,
whose shears end the lives of the wicked.
To her we offer our libations.

Now the smoking bowl is removed from next to the hole in the earth. As soon as it is gone, the leader of the worshippers pours wine into the opening in the altar, which flows directly into the denehold. The others watch then chant in unison:

Goddess, you have drunk our wine.
Appear to us, honoring our entreaties with your presence.
Grant one of us the strength to carry out your will
on the wicked ones who defile our world.
Goddess, prepare us for battle!

Somehow, the darkness of the cave seems to gather and become deeper around this scene: the kneeling supplicants, the smoke still boiling along the ground, and the hole in the earth which has just drunk the wine. Time ticks forward, as slow and inexorable as it has from the time of the ancient Greeks until this hour. But now something is rising from the deep passage in the ground to the surface of the cave and then up through the hole in the altar.

As this being rises above the surface of the tablet, the worshippers look on once again with awe: at the stiff spiked hair, the black dress tied at one shoulder while baring the other, the heavy eyebrows, the mouth painted a vivid red, and the blank eyes without pupil or iris. This is Atropos, the third of the Fates—the one called The Unturning: the cutter of the thread of life which her two sisters have already spun and measured.

She looks out at the darkness through eyes filled with darkness, for she is blind. And so nothing you can show her will turn her from her resolve—she is The Unturning, the Inflexible One. Who better to insist on the ways of Fate, beyond reasoning and moderation?

In her right hand, she holds a curious kind of shears or scissors.

These scissors are not made from two blades fastened together with a hinge, but from a single length of metal. They are ancient scissors, more simply and cleverly made than nowadays. The blades and the handle consist of one piece of metal: sharpened at the cutting edges, curved at the back to form the gripping place. The blades too are different. They are made to cut not only on the *inner* edges of the fulcrum, but on the *outer* edges as well—so this tool can act as both scissors and knife. And all four of the edges on the thing are razor-sharp.

When Atropos speaks, it is an eerie sound, her woman's voice echoing as though it comes from far away.

ATROPOS:
Tell me why you have summoned me from under the Earth
to these ancient caves, not so different from my home underground.
Fill my ears with your worship, you dangerous, secret men.
I think I know, from the time before now when you did so,
but I must hear it from your lips. It is part of the unbreakable law
that you or I must not question.
Goddesses and men alike must obey the ancient rules.
I can feel you shivering—though not from the coolness of this place.
Be brief! For my scissors are dry and thirsty.
Take care that you yourselves do not taste their light caress,
their gentle stroke of death, completed before you even realize
that your life is already ebbing away.

LEADER OF WORSHIPPERS:
Your words, goddess, freeze our hearts. Yet we know

our time is already measured, and what will be, will be.
And this makes us bold in our request.
Do not look upon us with anger—for we ask only to help you
perform your sacred and ancient duties.
The ground that has drunk blood wants more!
Great Atropos, The Unyielding—prepare us again to carry out your
will!

ATROPOS:
The gods listen to mortals, and help them when they can,
provided the ceremonies are worthy and offerings are made.
You have brought items that signify your sacrificial victims,
and you have poured the libation of wine.
I will permit this second action in my name.
The first one of you performed his deed successfully?

LEADER:
He did.

ATROPOS:
Where is he now?

LEADER:
He has gone away, as you said he must.

ATROPOS:
You have not seen him? He is truly gone?

LEADER:
He disappeared, as you instructed.

ATROPOS:
But not as you think, mortal. Yet it is not my duty to tell you more.
Hard lessons come unbidden to men and gods alike.

At this point, the child-goddess places her ancient scissors on the altar.

ATROPOS:
Here is your tool. As before, when I have descended to the underworld,
The one of you assigned this task will be chosen by a sign.
But take care, and remember this:
Afterwards, before he disappears, he must return
the scissors to this place—upon this altar—to be used again.
And hear this carefully, leader of my worshippers,
As I will not repeat it: choose your victims carefully from now on.
For I am not to be summoned every time you want to do this deed.
The sacrificial tool is yours as I grant it to you,
and permission to use it in my name.
As to the rest, it is the burden of you mortals to learn the price
of what you ask and perform. So be it, for I have spoken.

Whether the goddess descends again or simply disappears, none of the worshippers will know. They will realize, as they had from the first ceremony held here seven days ago, that there will be a moment of confusion, of thinning smoke from the dry ice, and an absence in the cave where a moment ago there had been a presence.

They will blink where they kneel, and try to clear their heads. And when their eyes focus again, they will see that one of them will be standing.

It is the sign.

CHAPTER 5

The Whitechapel Murders

jango Pierce-Jones, thought Scarlet, had as serious a look on his face as he was capable of. He was looking straight at Scarlet where the latter sat behind his desk in his office at the Yard, though Scarlet was sure his friend's mind was elsewhere.

It was the 10th of September—exactly one week since the Society's meeting, in which Pierce-Jones had burst in with the startling news of the man who had been found dismembered earlier that evening. Since then, a second woman's murder had occurred: that of Annie Chapman, who had been found two days ago in the backyard of 29 Hanbury Street in Spitalfields, and which had been officially logged in by the Yard's Inspector Joseph Chandler.

Scarlet and Pierce-Jones had been discussing the two cases.

"So, the divisional surgeon handled the autopsy in each case?" the latter asked now.

"Only in the second case, the Annie Chapman murder," Scarlet answered. "That was George Bagster Phillips of H Division, or the Whitechapel Division. In the first case, the Nichols woman, a Dr. Llewellyn was summoned from his home near the scene on Whitechapel Road around four that morning."

"Are you glad it wasn't you in either case?"

Scarlet understood his friend meant the mutilations of the victims, especially Annie Chapman, though 'glad' wasn't a word he'd have chosen.

"Yes, actually. It's not pleasant to see something like that, even for a police surgeon."

"The inquest began today in the Chapman case?"

Scarlet scarcely nodded. Apparently, he was as guilty as Pierce-Jones of going elsewhere in his thoughts in the midst of their conversation.

So there were two murders now, he was thinking. *Three*, if you counted the ghastly case of the man who appeared to have literally been ripped apart, as Pierce-Jones had reported to The Society. Two prostitutes in the East End, and a Norwegian labourer in Camberwell, two and a half miles from there in south London. The press was now calling the two East End killings the Whitechapel Murders.

The first victim: Mary Ann Nichols, found in Bucks Row, Whitechapel at 3.40 a.m. on 31 August.

And eight days later—two days ago on the eighth of September—Annie Chapman, whose body was discovered at 6.00 a.m. in the backyard of 29 Hanbury Street, Spitalfields, exactly one mile away.

Two women trapped in poverty and alcoholism who walked the streets to get their doss money each night. How many other prostitutes—London's 'unfortunates'—were in exactly the same straits? My God, thought Scarlet, how many more of them might be targets of this Whitechapel Murderer?

Scotland Yard, goaded by the press and by popular fear and outrage, was pulling out all the stops to put men on the street to uncover clues to the two grisly murders. Everyone was on edge; though people could still be seen out at night in the streets, markets, and alleyways of Whitechapel and Spitalfields. According to the many-headed monster Rumour, a foreigner had committed the murders. Or a Jew who lived in the neighborhood. No Englishman would commit such acts, the thinking went. By God, not only murdering women, but slicing open their stomachs with a knife and exposing their bowels!

Pierce-Jones had lit a cigar, and was pacing the floor in Scarlet's small office at the Yard, obviously still running things over in his mind. His friend watched him, waiting for the question or comment he knew was coming.

"About the Chapman woman . . . the second murder, two days ago Saturday. Did I understand from the stories in the press that there was some contention at the inquest today concerning the time of death?"

"Not a contention," Scarlet responded. "Say, a difference of opinion. Dr. Phillips, the divisional surgeon of H Division, arrived around 6.30 Saturday morning at the murder site. Since the body was cold, he stated that the Chapman woman had been dead at least a couple of hours. But, as was pointed out by Coroner Baxter himself, there are several reasons why the victim's body could have cooled more quickly than normal. For one thing, she was discovered lying on the ground in a backyard in the chill of early morning. Also, her clothes had been pushed up to reveal her abdomen—which was then opened up and exposed to the air. She'd also lost a considerable amount of blood. Any one of those factors alone would contribute to the body cooling much faster than normally."

"Meaning she was killed closer to the time she was found at 6.30 on Saturday morning?"

"Yes. Perhaps much closer. There's also the testimony of the landlady's son, John Richardson, concerning what he saw in the yard. Or more accurately, what he didn't see. His testimony is as conclusive as the body temperature in indicating that the woman was probably killed later than Phillips thought. Actually, I think it's more conclusive."

"Are you deliberately trying to be mysterious?"

Scarlet smiled apologetically. "Sorry, no. Richardson, the landlady's son, testified that he visits his mother's house in Hanbury Street for a look-round each morning on his way to work in Spitalfields Market. Apparently, some tools were stolen recently from the basement. He stated under oath that he visited the house between 4.45 and 4.50 that morning. He checked the cellar door, then walked through the hall passage from the front of the building to the back, then opened the door to the backyard. But rather than going down the steps into the yard, he sat down on the middle step— so that his feet were actually resting on the stone flags of the yard— and cut a piece of leather from his boot that was bothering him. Then he put his boot back on and left for his job in Spitalfields. . . . Do you see the contradiction in terms of the time of death?"

"You mean because the Chapman woman was found in that yard."

"Precisely. And not only in the yard," added Scarlet, "but within a few feet of the steps Richardson had been sitting on. It's a very small fenced-in yard, and he could hardly have missed seeing a bloodied corpse lying virtually at his feet if it had been there since 4.30, as Dr. Phillips believes."

"Which means Annie Chapman must have been murdered *after* 4.55 or 5.00 a.m., when Richardson got up from the steps and left for work."

"That's right. Meaning just an hour or so before her body was found."

Pierce-Jones thought about this piece of information. "So, what you're saying, Will, is that it was a very close thing in terms of the murderer not being seen."

"Oh, a *very* close thing," his friend agreed. "The house at No. 29 Hanbury is a three-story tenement, with six families living there. There's even a cat's meat shop in the storefront of the house on the Hanbury Street side."

He leaned forward to speak directly to Pierce-Jones.

"Now, consider what must have happened. The murderer apparently accompanied Annie Chapman from where she picked him up on the street and through the interior hall from the front to the back of the building. The front door was always left unlocked, by the way, because of all the people who lived in the building going back and forth at all hours. The prostitutes in the area must have known that they could get into the building, and then through a dark passage leading to the backyard, where they could conduct business privately."

"So, you're saying that the house and yard were a known place for these women to ply their trade?" asked Django.

"Almost certainly," replied Scarlet. "From what the Yard has been able to gather, the residents even ignored seeing people in the hall at night or the early hours of the morning. They had no idea whether these people were strangers or relatives of the other residents of the building."

"Yes, I can see that."

"But think about it," Scarlet insisted. "The killer—let's call him the Whitechapel Murderer as the papers are doing—took an awful chance. He walked through the hallway of a crowded tenement building with his victim, then slit her throat in a small backyard—so small that he had to leave her corpse near the foot of the steps leading into the yard. Then he lifted up her clothes and sliced open her abdomen, placing part of her intestines over her right shoulder. He did all this when it was already daylight, with people able to look down on him from the second or third floors if they had been at the windows, and with the residents of the house already rising to get to early jobs in the markets."

"He'd have had to work very fast then, wouldn't he?" the other asked. "Which means he had to know what he was doing in terms of human anatomy."

"Maybe," Scarlet hedged. "There's already disagreement among us doctors about that. We could, for instance, be looking for a butcher or someone who works in the fish markets."

Pierce-Jones thought about that, then added an observation of his own to Scarlet's scenario:

"And after the murder, of course, he had to make his way back through the hallway to the front of the house and then along Hanbury Street, where any early risers would obviously notice a man covered in blood. What about hopping the fence to escape through another yard?"

"Well, the fence wouldn't be a problem. But then he'd have the difficulty of fleeing through one of the other houses to get to the street. And none of them have the long interior hallway that No. 29 does."

The next question was an obvious one from a member of The Society.

"Do you think there's a supernatural element to what happened, especially in the second murder? Given this miraculous escape, I mean."

"I haven't the slightest idea," answered Scarlet. "The killer could have just been lucky. It's happened before."

"And the Yard hasn't found any clues?"

"None. Nothing left at the crime scenes or bloody handprints or footprints. And of course, no sightings of the killer that any citizens can tell us about."

"So we don't know where and when he'll strike again . . . and whether he'll be this lucky the next time."

Scarlet considered that statement. Then he said:

"It doesn't seem likely though, does it? There was something about the inevitability of his being caught in a story I read recently concerning the first murder, of Mary Ann Nichols on August thirty-first. I think it was in either the *Tower Hamlets Independent* or the *East End Local Advertiser*. The paper thought there was little doubt that the perpetrator will be captured. It said something like, 'A lunatic of this sort can scarcely remain at large for any length of time in the teeming neighbourhood of Whitechapel.'"

"So, you believe it's only a matter of time before this man is caught?"

"I would think so," answered Scarlet. Then he added: "Given the nature of these crimes, I certainly hope so."

CHAPTER 6

A Quiet Death, to Start With

t is now ten-thirty on the night of Monday, the 10th of September, and the streets of the East End are relatively quiet. The crowds that congregated outside of No. 29 Hanbury Street yesterday, out of curiosity about the house and backyard where poor Annie Chapman was found murdered and mutilated on Saturday morning, have gone. After their conversation earlier this evening in Dr. Scarlet's office at Scotland Yard (which we have just listened in on), he and Django Pierce-Jones have gone to dinner.

We are now on New Road, between Commercial Road and Charlotte Street in Whitechapel. The sidewalks on this particular block are empty this late in the evening except for two entities: a man named George Ross, and Revenge, which is coming up fast behind George on silent wings.

George feels the wind from the wings above him, moving in the same direction he is walking. Even if he had an imaginative mind (which he does not), George would probably still have put the sensation down to a sudden breeze at his back. And so he does. Death is now in front of him rather than behind him. But it hardly matters.

George may be unimaginative, but he has a fiercely loyal disposition. He believes in Queen and country. To those two poles of his life, and to the organization which he feels deserves his allegiance, he is steadfast and brave and a boon companion. His loyalty is in fact the reason he is about to die, though he wouldn't understand the connection if you explained it to him.

George Ross is a costermonger or street vendor of oysters and eels. His territory is south Whitechapel near the Thames, and Limehouse, which is even closer to the river, and he is a good provider for his wife and two daughters. He is short, stocky, and strong, though his strength is pitiful compared to what he is about to face.

He is a 46-year-old East Ender who is red in the face (he has just drunk two pints of Whitbread porter too many), and now as he heads homeward is looking for a place to relieve himself. George understands why his gait is slightly unsteady. But for the life of him (however much is left in his remaining minutes), he can't understand why he is seeing what is apparently in front of him.

He is approaching the Whitechapel Mission, a low dirty-brick building with a large weathered wooden cross on the wall facing George. Perched on the roof of the Mission—right there above the entrance!—are three enormous birds.

But George thinks: is *that* what they are? No, he decides: these are much too large to be birds. As insane as the thought is, they're more like women with feathers and huge wings on their backs. They are sitting up there, quite still, gripping the edge of the roof with long sharp talons, and he can swear that they're watching his progress as he approaches the building.

As George stumbles closer, he realizes why he thought these were women. They have women's faces, these birds: old and wrinkled and angry-looking. One of them—the one in the middle—cranes her neck forward a bit, as if to look more closely at *him*, and slightly lifts and resettles her wings . . . and George pees in his pants without realizing it.

Now he halts in the middle of the street and calls himself an ass who drinks too much—which is something he needs to bloody well *stop* if this is what he's seeing. He doesn't even realize that the bird-women are gone from their perch until he feels something scratch across his throat. Scratch . . . is that the word? No, the word is *slice*, for he feels something wet soaking his collar and realizes that it's his own blood.

"What in hell is happening?" he wonders, as his knees buckle and he finds himself on the ground, lying on the paving stones on his left side without the strength to get up again. Then he hears wings beating fiercely around his head.

Bit by bit, George's world is ripped away.

And not only his world.

CHAPTER 7

An Investigation Begins

itting on his garden patio in the late September afternoon, William Scarlet had a ridiculous thought. It suddenly occurred to him that, of the 30,000 or so physicians currently practicing in England and Wales, he was lucky in not being one of the two who had been pulled into the pair of Whitechapel Murders.

The odds in this calculation were entirely logical. But they had nothing whatever to do with his feelings in the matter.

There were two reasons behind his sense of gratitude.

First, as he had told Pierce-Jones, being the doctor summoned to declare death at the scene of a mutilation murder, and then to carry out the post-mortem, was not a pleasant experience. These duties had fallen to Dr. Llewellyn (the Nichols killing), and Dr. Phillips (the Chapman murder).

Second, not being officially part of Scotland Yard's Whitechapel Murders investigation left him free in his spare time to pursue the separate inquiry The Society of Supernatural and Psychic Research had decided to undertake. As unlikely as it may seem, that inquiry concerned entirely different murders that also involved mutilation of the victim.

There were two of these "other" killings now. The first had been the violent death and dismemberment of the Norwegian labourer

Anders Haugen that Pierce-Jones had reported to the Society the night of the meeting of September third. The second death, that of a street peddler named George Ross, had occurred a week later.

The latter case had been similar to the first one: remains were found of a man (Ross), who had somehow been torn to pieces. Only the widespread fear in the East End of a fiend hunting down Whitechapel prostitutes, and the press frenzy associated with it, had kept the grisly murders of these two men out of the news. That, and the fact that only one of the men's deaths had occurred in Whitechapel—one of the two districts of the prostitutes' murders—while the other had taken place in the borough of Southwark, two-and-a-half miles away and south of the river.

The Society's interest in these cases rather than the Whitechapel Murders was also logical. If any events in a suddenly bloody London had a supernatural connection, it was likely to be the men's murders, not the women's. Though the Whitechapel murderer had so far been ghost-like in his invisibility and skill in not leaving a single clue, the manner of the killings was easily understood: they resulted from a sharp knife in an assured hand. It was simply a case of overpowering the victim, slitting her throat, then slicing open the abdomen to reveal and remove a section of bowel.

A grisly modus operandi, of course, and indescribably cruel. But at the same time comprehensible to any doctor or even a layman.

But what about men who were *pulled apart piece by piece*? Did that even describe it? 'Ripped apart' or 'sliced apart,' would do equally well—because a cause of dismemberment that was both powerful and sharp had been evident. In his capacity as Assistant Chief Surgeon at Scotland Yard, Scarlet had examined the men's remains. He had chosen not to view the bodies of the Whitechapel women, as the descriptions given in the inquests by Dr. Llewellyn, and by the divisional police surgeon Dr. Phillips, had been precise and quite sufficient.

It was evident from his examination that whatever had attacked the two men wasn't a man with a knife underneath his butcher's apron or frock coat. These killings were *outré*, something that violated the norms even of murder.

The army of policemen and citizen volunteers searching for the Whitechapel Murderer were necessary and would do their duty. But somehow, Scarlet didn't think they had any part to play in the search for this particular fiend. This was The Society's territory. Its interest in the case was altogether fitting and proper, as the American president Lincoln had said in his famous address twenty-five years ago.

The door from the kitchen opening behind him and a voice asking "All quiet, then?" banished these thoughts from his mind.

Pierce-Jones took his accustomed seat at the patio table. It was the one that gave him a view of the kitchen, and any tea or pastries that Scarlet's cook and housekeeper Mrs. Bennie might be preparing.

"It's been two weeks since a man was last torn apart," answered Scarlet, "and two-and-a-half weeks since the last woman was murdered in Whitechapel. I'd say that peace has broken out conspicuously all over London."

Given the serious expression on his friend's face despite what might be taken as light-hearted remarks, Django chose not to respond.

Scarlet checked to see if there was enough tea left to pour a cup for both of them, and found that there was. He always insisted that Mrs. Bennie include service for two when she made tea. Django was apt to show up unannounced at any time. As he just had, in fact.

"How was surgery today?"

As money was not an issue for Scarlet, he only scheduled private patients in his home-based surgery in the mornings and early afternoons. Late afternoons were taken up either by a visit to his office at Scotland Yard or time in the garden behind his house. Today, the garden had won out.

"The usual," he replied distractedly. "A normal mixture of

everyday complaints, thank goodness." After hardly a pause, he said: "What do we have to go on concerning the men?" As in any investigation, the background and last-known movements of the victim were of paramount importance.

"Very little," replied Pierce-Jones. "We have two men who seem to have led quite ordinary lives. No criminal record in either case, nor anything suspicious in terms of friends or associates. Both were hard-working types who did their jobs and then went home to their families. Maybe a visit to the local for a pint or two first.

"We know that Haugen worked at a haulage company on the Peckham Road in Camberwell near where he lived, loading and unloading wagons. He was a big, strong bloke from what everyone says, just the type a haulage concern would need."

"And the location where he was found?" Scarlet asked.

"About a mile and a half from his place of business."

"Where he'd gone for a walk that day."

"According to his wife."

"Plausible?"

"I think so," said Django. "There are playing pitches in Green Dale Fields where he was found, with areas of long grass and trees surrounding them. It would be a pleasant place for a walk in the evening after work, I would think."

"No evidence of any place he visited prior to going there—a pub, for instance?"

Pierce-Jones shook his head. "And we probably won't find any. He was well enough known in his neighborhood that people would have recognized him and been able to tell us afterward."

"How about the crime location . . . any witnesses who saw him meeting anyone in the park?"

"Not that we've found. Fisher and Trippel* have been helping me in my inquiries. We've turned up nothing yet at all."

---

* Two young members of the Society.

"And what about George Ross, the second victim?" asked Scarlet.

"Basically, the same story . . . though a pub does figure in this time. Rather prominently, I'd say," added Django. "Plenty of witnesses at the Hare and Hounds, where he was drinking. Apparently, he was soused."

"I know," said Scarlet. "I could smell it on the remains. You wouldn't think that would be the case." He shrugged, and added: "Actually, I suppose you would. If you can smell it on the breath and coming out of the pores of a man who is dead drunk when alive, why should it be any different on the body parts you're examining?"

"That's a charming thought."

Scarlet went on as if he hadn't heard. "So, the man was drunk that night. But nothing else in terms of bad behavior or running with the wrong crowd?"

"Absolutely not, I'd say. George Ross was apparently a hard-working street vendor who provided for his family and was a good citizen. Did fairly well with his oyster cart and brought all of his profits home—except for what he set aside for drink, which probably wasn't much. He was on his way home on a typical evening after work when . . . whatever it was overtook him."

Scarlet let all of that sink in. Then he gave voice to the uneasiness he was feeling.

"What are we dealing with here, Django? What is it that attacks two family men in the heart of London and literally rips them apart, then escapes without being seen or even heard? What could cause such mayhem and not be spotted? And why these two men?"

"You just said, '*what*,' not 'who,'" the other observed.

"I did, didn't I?" agreed Scarlet. He thought for a moment, then added: "It's the wounds."

"Meaning?"

"Meaning, that's what's unusual concerning the deaths of these two men. Among other things. But at least, that's a good place to start."

"What about the wounds?"

"They're inconsistent. There are deep puncture wounds in the abdominal areas of both men—I mean the parts of the abdomen that were identifiable as such. But the other wounds, the ones that resulted in the small pieces of flesh we found, are tearing wounds. What we doctors call an avulsion—when the tissue is forcibly torn away from the body. But that too is puzzling."

"Why?" asked Django.

"Because the edges of the tissue were *incised*—cleanly sliced, I mean—by some sharp edge. Almost as though a surgical instrument was used. That's inconsistent with the forceful tearing of the flesh."

"Do you mean that more than one instrument was used?"

"I'm not sure if it *was* an instrument," answered Scarlet. "For instance, some of the wounds are consistent with an attack from an animal."

"I had that thought as well," said Django. "But what kind of animal?"

"That's just it," replied Scarlet. "There's no animal in London that could make those wounds . . . or the British Isles, for that matter. Probably not even in most of Europe. In Africa, maybe, or parts of India."

"What about an animal that escaped from a zoo?"

"Perhaps. Or there's another possibility: that someone recently shipped such a creature into London from abroad."

"Yes, of course," agreed Django Pierce-Jones. "That should be relatively easy to uncover, shouldn't it?"

"Let's find out," replied Scarlet.

But their research uncovered no escapes of any specimens from a zoo, and nothing out of the ordinary in terms of importation of animals into Greater London. It seemed that both investigations— Scotland Yard's search for the Whitechapel Murderer, and The Society's probe into the dismemberment of the two men—were stalled.

In just a few days, however, the Whitechapel murders would roar back to life, in a display of horror that was literally doubled from what had gone before. And a continuation of the other bout of savagery wouldn't be far behind.

But before all of that, someone with a cruel mind had something to say to the authorities and the rest of the world.

CHAPTER 8

Yours Truly, Jack the Ripper

he letter was dated 25 September 1888, and was stamped with an East Central London postmark. It was addressed to 'The Boss, Central News Office, London City,' where it was delivered on 27 September. Despite the lurid associations, the red handwriting on the two sheets of plain paper inside the envelope was from ink, not blood.

By this time, nearly a month after Mary Ann Nichols's murder and two and a half weeks after Annie Chapman's, the police, press, and notable public figures had received a sea of letters purporting to give information on the Whitechapel Murderer. The frenzy created by the newspapers seemingly led to everyone wanting to be in on the now-famous investigation.

But this letter was different—and for the first time, the supposed killer gave himself a name. It read as follows:

25 Sept. 1888.

Dear Boss

I keep on hearing the police
have caught me but they wont fix

me just yet. I have laughed when
they look so clever and talk about
being on the <u>right</u> track. That joke
about Leather Apron gave me real
fits. I am down on whores and
I shant quit ripping them til I
do get buckled. Grand work the last
job was. I gave the lady no time to
squeal. How can they catch me now.
I love my work and want to start
again. You will soon hear of me
with my funny little games. I
saved some of the proper <u>red</u> stuff in
a ginger beer bottle over the last job
to write with but it went thick
like glue and I cant use it. Red
ink is fit enough I hope. <u>ha. ha.</u>
The next job I do I shall clip
the lady's ears off and send to the
police officers just for jolly wouldn't
you. Keep this letter back till I
do a bit more work then give
it out straight. My knife's so nice
and sharp I want to get to work

right away if I get a chance.
Good luck.

> *Yours truly,*
> *Jack the Ripper*

Don't mind me giving the trade name
wasnt good enough to post this before
I got all the red ink off my hands
curse it.
No luck yet. They say Im a doctor
now ha ha

'Leather Apron' referred to a man much feared by the East End prostitutes, who wore an apron and had been frightening them for some time. He was identified by the police and ruled out as the murderer.

The Central News Agency considered the letter a prank and didn't send it along to Scotland Yard until two days later. Scarlet, his mind still fixed on the animal-like wounds found on the two murdered men, happened to be at No. 5, Whitehall Place—the building containing his office and the Yard's post-mortem facilities—when the letter was received next door at No. 4, Whitehall Place, the original location of Metropolitan Police headquarters.

The police decided that the letter was a hoax and took no action. In their minds, there was nothing in this taunting note but the fact that a narcissist was capitalizing on the series of crimes by giving himself a catchy new name.

In just a few hours, however, the self-mocking "funny little games" the writer mentioned would begin again, reaching a new level of ferocity.

And the catchy new name would become legendary.

CHAPTER 9

Forty-Five Minutes of Hell

aturday, the 29th of September 1888, was a dull and cloudy day in London, with the temperature reaching a high of 68 degrees Fahrenheit. Rain began at 9.05 p.m. and lasted until after midnight. A total of 0.242 inches of rain fell. It was a typically gloomy London day that hung heavily on the city, and anyone with an equally gloomy imagination could envision it leading to murder as the clock struck midnight.

The Whitechapel Murderer (or, if one preferred now, Jack the Ripper) obliged, and quickly, too. By 1.44 a.m. that morning of the 30th, two more of the East End's "unfortunates" lay in pools of their own blood. If only the second woman of the two was horribly disfigured, it was almost certainly because the murderer had been interrupted in his work in the first of his attacks that morning.

It had been twenty-two days since the last victim, Annie Chapman, had been found in the backyard of 29 Hanbury Street on Saturday, the 8th of September. The fact that this time, the phantom of Whitechapel killed twice in the same early morning was one of two anomalies concerning the September 30 killings. The second unusual fact was that one of the murders occurred not in Whitechapel, but just over that borough's border separating it from the City of London. The City is a county and local government designation of its own, encompassing the financial and central business districts of London and many of its historic sites.

The City also has its own police force. For the first time, then, that force joined The Metropolitan Police or Scotland Yard in pursuing the serial murderer of London's prostitutes.

The peculiar schedule and state of mind of the killer led him on this early morning, first, to Berner Street in Whitechapel (in the jurisdiction of the Metropolitan Police's H division), then to Mitre Square in the City, which is located a half-mile west of Whitechapel. Both murder sites were secluded from the streets they were situated on, and each must have seemed to the murderer to be a relatively hidden place for his work. The presence of a man and his cart apparently interrupted that work in the first instance, however. Only in Mitre Square— less than an hour later and a mere half-mile away—did the killer find the time and privacy he needed to carry out his full intentions.

The double killing, along with the invitation for the City force to join in hunting him down, made it seem as though the murderer was now taunting the police. And for the first time, there were witnesses who may have seen the killer.

These third and fourth murders—this time *within less than an hour of each other*—combined with a bodily mutilation more horrific than anything that had come before, was enough to put London's population into a frenzy.

And it did.

RIPPER VICTIM #3: ELIZABETH STRIDE

She was originally from Sweden and was known as "Long Liz," even though she was only somewhere between five feet two- and five inches tall. Perhaps it had something to do with her last name. It was said that she was only an occasional prostitute or "dollymop" ("dolly" being a slang term for penis). Otherwise, she worked as a charwoman.

Depending upon who you asked, she was either missing the teeth in her lower left jaw, or all of her upper front teeth. Like the Ripper's victims before her, drink had helped ruin her life. Her last known address was a common lodging house at 32 Flower and Dean Street in Whitechapel. She was 44 years old.

On the night of 29-30 September 1888, she was dressed in a cheap black dress of imitation satin—a fabric called "sateen"—and a velveteen bodice which had faded from black to brown and which was, in fact, constructed of imitation velvet. She had on white stockings and ankle-length boots. Over her dress and bodice, she wore a long black jacket trimmed with fur. Topping all of this was a black crepe bonnet which had been stuffed with newspaper for a better fit. On her jacket was pinned a red rose.

By the early morning of the 30th, Long Liz's street walking had taken her to the vicinity of Dutfield Yard, in Berner Street, Whitechapel, the site of a cart builder. Dutfield had moved his business elsewhere, but his sign remained, including a large wagon wheel fastened above the gate of the yard which was easily visible from the street.

Located within the small yard was the International Working Men's Educational Club or IWME, a socialist organization made up mainly of Russian and Polish Jews. But the yard itself was poorly lit; and any light from the upper story of the club fell not on the ground but on the cottages opposite. To avoid having to knock on the front door of the club's premises on Berner Street, members typically left the gate to the yard open, so they could get into the building by a side entrance or via the kitchen door in the back. It was on the short path between the gate and the back entrance to the club that Elizabeth Stride's body was found.

The attack which severed the blood vessels in Long Liz's throat also cut through her windpipe, preventing her from calling out to alert anyone in this confined area. She probably took as long as a minute and a half to bleed to death, because only the blood vessels on the left side of her throat had been severed. She was almost certainly forced to the ground before her throat was slit, as the blood gushing from the wound flowed down to the pavement and not onto her clothes. From there, it trickled down the yard toward the back door of the club.

The proximity of the social organization to the murder site was the reason Stride's body was found quickly, by a man coming through the gateway with his pony cart. And although this discovery prevented the murderer from any further outrage on the corpse, it was, ironically, only a few minutes too late to save her.

The timing of events, as reconstructed from testimony at the inquest, is as follows:

12.10 a.m. — Club member William West steps out of the club's side door to drop off a job at the printing office where he works on the other side of the yard. He glances toward the gates as he walks across the enclosed yard but sees nothing suspicious. He returns to the club by the same side door, then he and his brother set out for home. They leave the front entrance on Berner Street at about 12.15 a.m.

12.30 a.m. — Joseph Lave, who is lodging at the club on a visit from America, steps into the street from the front entrance to get a breath of fresh air. He is there about ten minutes, but sees nothing out of the ordinary on Berner Street. He goes back inside the club at around 12.40 a.m.

12.40 a.m. — At approximately the same time, Morris Eagle, the chairman of the debate held at the club that night, returns from having walked a female friend home. He finds the street door locked and goes around to the Dutfield Yard gate. The gates are wide open, which is not unusual, as members use the gateway to enter the back of the club through the unlocked doors.

As Eagle enters the yard, he can hear a friend singing in Russian through the open first-floor windows. His approach to the building takes him over the exact spot—on the pathway next to the wall on the right— where Elizabeth Stride's body will be found only twenty minutes later at 1.00 a.m. If the body had been there at 12.40, Eagle would certainly have seen it, perhaps even tripped over it. But nothing is there at this time. He enters the club by the side door.

1.00 a.m. — A man named Louis Diemschutz turns his wheel-barrow-and-pony cart into Dutfield's Yard through the open gate. Diemschutz is the club steward who also sells costume jewelry. Every Saturday night, he offers his wares at Westow Hill, near Crystal Palace Park, and he is now returning with his unsold goods.

He sees no one in the yard. His pony, however, does. The pony shies to the left a few steps in from the gate; and looking into the darkness, Diemschutz sees something on the ground on the right. He prods it and tries to lift it with the handle of his whip. He gets down and strikes a match. Then he is running into the club and asking for his wife, afraid that she might have seen the body and become frightened. "There's a woman lying in the yard but I cannot say whether she's drunk or dead," he says.

But Long Liz won't be drunk anymore.

WITNESSES

For the first time in the Whitechapel Murders, there were witnesses who saw one of the murder victims— and equally important, the man she was with. This was the first victim that morning: Elizabeth Stride. The witnesses song Long Liz in the company of a man shortly before her death. Three of them described this man as follows:

PC William Smith 452H. At 12.35 a.m. while on his beat, Police Constable Smith noticed a man and woman talking in Berner Street. The woman had a red rose pinned to her coat; and later, upon viewing the body, Smith identified Liz Stride as the woman wearing that coat. The man was around five feet seven inches tall, with a dark complexion and a small moustache. He wore a black "diagonal," i.e., cutaway coat, a hard felt hat, and had on a white collar and tie. PC Smith reported that he did not hear any of the couple's conversation.

Israel Schwartz, of 22, Helen Street, Backchurch Lane. Schwartz testified that at 12.45, he turned into Berner Street from Commercial Road. When he reached the gateway to Dutfield's Yard, he noticed a man speaking to a woman who was standing in the gateway. The man appeared to be about 30 years of age, five feet five inches tall, with dark hair, a small brown moustache, and broad shoulders.

This man was dressed in dark jacket and trousers, and wore a black peaked cap on his head. The man tried to pull the woman into the street, then pushed her down on the footway. She screamed three times, but not loudly.

As Schwartz crossed to the opposite side of the street, he saw a second man standing nearby and lighting his pipe. The man who had thrown the woman down yelled "Lipski!" to the other man. As Schwartz walked away, he noticed that the second man was following him. He began running along Berner Street, and the man left off the chase. Whether 'Lipski' was the second man's name, or intended as a derogatory term for the Jewish Schwartz, is not known.

William Marshall, labourer residing at 64, Berner Street, Commercial Road. On Sunday, 30 September, Mr. Marshall viewed the body of a deceased woman in the mortuary, stating that it was the same woman [Stride] he saw talking to a man on Saturday evening, three doors down from where he lives in Berner Street. When questioned by Coroner Wynne Baxter at the Stride inquest, he testified as follows:

Coroner: Was she wearing a flower when you saw her?
Marshall: No
Coroner: Were they talking quietly?
Marshall: Yes.
Coroner: Can you describe the man?
Marshall: There was no lamp near, and I did not see the face of the man she was talking to. He had on a small black coat and dark trousers. He seemed to me to be a middle-aged man.
Coroner: What sort of cap was he wearing?
Marshall: A round cap with a small peak to it; something like what a sailor would wear.
Coroner: What height was he?
Marshall: About 5 foot 6 inches, and he was rather stout. He was decently dressed, and I should say he worked at some light business, and had more the appearance of a clerk than anything else.
Coroner: You are quite sure this is the woman?
Marshall: Yes, I am. I did not take much notice of them. I was standing at my door, and what attracted my attention first was her standing there some time,

and he was kissing her. I heard the man say to deceased, "You would say anything but your prayers," and she laughed. He was mild speaking, and appeared to be an educated man. They went down the street.

Coroner: Were either of them the worse for drink?

Marshall: They did not appear to be so. I went in about 12 o'clock and heard nothing more until I heard "Murder" being called in the street. It had then just gone 1 o'clock.

RIPPER VICTIM #4: CATHERINE ("KATE") EDDOWES

Only forty-five minutes later and a mere half-mile away, another victim was discovered. This time, the killing had occurred in Mitre Square, which is just within the bounds of the City—the only borough with its own police force, which was separate from the Metropolitan Police or Scotland Yard.

This time, London was given a display of savagery and boldness that fairly took its collective breath away.

Mitre Square was a large yard of 120 feet square, which was bounded by business establishments, houses, and warehouses. The principal entrance to it was a carriageway leading into it from Mitre Street. There was also a covered court, about twenty yards log, leading from St. James's Place at the northwest corner, and a passage of thirty yard's length known as Church Passage slightly to the east of that which also gave entrance.

The Square itself was a busy enclosure during the hours of commerce because of the businesses that backed up on it; but it was deserted and in almost complete darkness at night. The houses located there were either empty or in poor condition, though interestingly enough, a City policeman—PC Richard Pearce—lived in one of them with his family.

Among the close calls that the murderer experienced that morning was the passing by of two policemen within four or five minutes of each other. Had the first constable entered Mitre Square instead of just walking by, he might have caught the killer in the act. That was PC James Harvey, who at 1.41 a.m. was walking on Church Passage. Seeing nothing unusual, he continued on his way. But had he done more than take a quick glance into the Square, he may have surprised the killer at work on the still-warm body of his victim.

The other policeman was PC Edward Watkins, whose regular patrol took him past Mitre Square at 1.45 a.m. Unlike PC Harvey, Watkins entered the Square, where the light from his Bull's Eye belt lantern revealed the body of a woman lying in a pool of blood. Like the other victims, her throat had been cut, and her clothes had been pushed above her waist. The wounds to her abdomen were fearsome. They were deep enough, in fact, that her bowels protruded.

City Police officers didn't carry whistles, so Watkins enlisted the help of George Morris, a former policeman himself who was now the night-watchman at a tea warehouse in the Square.
"For God's sake, man, come out and assist me,"

Watkins pleaded with the other man. "Another woman has been ripped open."

It was Morris who ran to nearby Aldgate to fetch some additional police officers. Only later would the night-watchman think how odd it was that he hadn't heard a sound as the murder had taken place. As he put it: "As a rule I can hear the footstep of the policeman as he passes by every quarter of an hour, so the woman could not have uttered any cry without my detecting it.

"It was only last night," he went on, "that I made the remark to some policeman that I wished the butcher would come around Mitre Square, and I would soon give him a doing, and here, to be sure, he has come and I was perfectly ignorant of it."

Catherine Eddowes, the latest victim, was another of the East End's "unfortunates"—a woman whose life was circumscribed by broken relationships, poverty, drink, and the too-common result of those three: prostitution.

The clothing on the small, almost painfully thin woman killed in Mitre Square and who now lay on the mortuary table stamped her immediately as either a vagrant or someone who lived in one of the common lodging houses. The clothes were worn and dirty: a black cloth jacket with imitation fur on the collar, a dark-green skirt topped by a man's white waistcoat, and a red silk scarf around her neck. She wore brown ribbed stockings, mended at the feet with white cloth, and a pair of men's boots. Underneath it all were a petticoat, an alpaca skirt, a tattered blue skirt, and a white calico chemise. A black straw bonnet of green and black velvet and black beads completed her outfit. She looked to be around forty years old, and was five feet tall.

The authorities' efforts at identification were aided by a blue tattoo of 'T.C.' on her left forearm. That turned out to be the initials of a man named Thomas Conway, who "Kate" Eddowes had met in the City of Birmingham and begun living with when she was sixteen. Though they never married, the couple stayed together for twenty-two years and had three children. The publicity given by the press to the murderer's as-yet unidentified fourth victim had brought out the man Kate had been living with in one of the lodging houses for the past seven years: John Kelly. Her name, he told the authorities, was Kate Conway alias Kelly.

The police eventually identified her as Catherine Eddowes: a woman said to be the most likeable of the Ripper's victims, yet one whose life was marred by excessive drinking and, at least once, theft against her domestic employer. Kelly had last seen her the day before, and as it happened, he was worried about her safety. As Kelly remembered afterwards, Kate had promised to be home early. Her last words to him were:

"Don't you fear for me. I'll take care of myself and I shan't fall into his hands."

Kate had actually been in a police holding cell at Bishopsgate Street Police Station due to public intoxication up until less than an hour prior to her death. Once sobered up, she was released by PC George Hutt. When she asked him what time it was, he replied: "Too late for you to get any more drink."

As Kate was leaving, Hutt asked her to shut the door behind her.

"All right," Eddowes replied. "Good night, old cock."

From the police station, Mitre Square was an eight-minute walk southeast.

THE AUTOPSY OF CATHERINE EDDOWES

Thus, in the first hours of Sunday, the thirtieth of September, two new major investigations were being carried out by two separate police forces. The Metropolitan Police had added Elizabeth Stride's death in Dutfield's Yard to their growing roster of Ripper cases, while the City of London police were coming to terms with the outrage that had been perpetrated on the body of Catherine Eddowes in Mitre Square.

Now for the first time, William Scarlet became involved.

At the request of Sir Edward Mallinson, M.D., Chief Surgeon of the Metropolitan Police and Scarlet's boss, the City Police allowed Scarlet to be present at Catherine Eddowes's autopsy. The post-mortem was carried out by Dr. Frederick Gordon Brown, surgeon of the City of London Police Force, who had also been called to the murder scene.

Brown mentioned to Scarlet before the autopsy began that the body as discovered in Mitre Square had exhibited a 10 ½-long cut through the skirt and abdomen. A large segment of the intestines, smeared with fecal matter, had been pulled out and placed over the right shoulder, while a separate section about 2 feet long had been detached from the body and placed between the torso and the left arm.

As the bloody clothes were carefully removed at the Golden Lane mortuary, a piece of the deceased's ear dropped out of the clothing. Now the formal post-mortem began. As he proceeded, Dr. Brown continuously described what he was seeing, as one of the other doctors present took notes. The gist of those notes is as follows:

THE FACE: Apart from a wide incision in the throat which immediately drew attention, the face, as Dr. Brown put it, "was very much mutilated." There were horizontal and vertical cuts present all over the face and the right ear—17 of them by Dr. Brown's count—from both eyelids down to the chin. An especially deep cut extended over the bridge of the nose and down to the jaw on the right side. This cut reached the bone and "divided all the structures of the cheek except the mucous membrane of the mouth." A half-inch at the tip of the nose was missing.

THE THROAT: The cause of death was a deep incision in the throat which extended 6 or 7 inches in length, severing the large vessels on the left side of the neck and reaching the intervertebral cartilages. Death occurred at once, and the mutilations to the body took place immediately afterwards.

THE ABDOMEN: The front walls of the abdomen were laid open from the breast bone to the pubes. The abdominal walls were divided, beginning opposite the ensiform cartilage [at the bottom of the sternum], and continuing downward to the right side of the vagina and rectum. The liver was stabbed with a sharp instrument.

The skin was retracted through the whole of the cut in the abdomen but the vessels were not clotted—nor had there been any appreciable bleeding from the vessel. Dr. Brown drew the conclusion from this fact that the long cut was made after death, and that there would consequently not be much blood on the murderer.

He stated that, "The cut was made by someone on the right side of the body kneeling below the middle of the body." The peritoneum or lining of the abdominal cavity was cut through on the left side and the left kidney removed—Dr. Brown's opinion was that, "someone who knew the position of the kidney must have done it." The womb was cut through horizontally, leaving a stump of ¾ of an inch; the rest of the womb had been taken away.

It was the doctor's opinion that one assailant had done all of this. He felt sure that there was no struggle—that the throat had been so quickly cut through that the victim would not have been able to utter a sound. The murder and mutilation would have taken at least five minutes, and "the perpetrator of this act had sufficient time or he would not have nicked the lower eyelids." The wounds on the face, he thought, had been done to disfigure the corpse.

The actual notes entered into the case book were much more specific than this, leading Scarlet to think that Dr. Brown's post-mortem had been both professional and thorough. But he couldn't stop thinking of a different, much more colloquial description of the victim: that of Police Constable Watkins who had discovered the body.

"She was ripped up like a pig in the market," he had told the press.

THE UNLIKELY ESCAPE

The Eddowes murder exceeded in brutality and depravity anything yet exhibited by the Whitechapel Ghost or Ripper. None of the other three women had been butchered like this. The killer's escape during this early morning mayhem, however, seemed just as remarkable—even otherworldly.

He had begun laying his trail of blood shortly after midnight, on what was now September 30th, in Berner Street in Whitechapel.

In the dark of Dutfield's Yard—in a space that measured only eighteen feet from a busy gateway behind him to the kitchen door of the IWME club in front of him—he had slit Elizabeth Stride's throat.

So close an affair was it in terms of people coming and going, however, that the murderer had worked within a scant twenty-minute window, when only luck had allowed him not to be seen. Or was it only luck? In the event, he only had time to kill instantly and no more—as the arrival of a man in a pony cart had prevented any mutilation of this victim.

Was the killer, in fact, still kneeling beside Long Liz's body when Mr. Diemschutz arrived with his cart? And if he was, how did he successfully escape from such a small and crowded yard as Dutfield's?

Liz's body was found at 1.00 a.m. The killer then fled from a Whitechapel now aroused and alarmed at a third prostitute's murder only a half-block from busy Commercial Road. One would think that the monster would leave the borough—as indeed he did—but not that he would cross into the City and commit a second murder and vicious mutilation less than forty-five minutes later. Knowing that the Metropolitan Police and citizen vigilante groups were on the trail behind him, why would he invite the participation of a *second* police force—the City Police—immediately afterwards?

The murderer's actions became even more inexplicable over the next hour and a quarter. At the very time that Dr. Brown was examining the second victim of the morning—Catherine Eddowes— at 2.20 a.m., a Whitechapel policeman, PC Alfred Long, was patrolling Goulston Street, about 350 yards north of Mitre Square. He noticed nothing unusual.

However, when his regular patrol brought him back to the spot at 2.50 a.m., he found something extraordinary: a folded piece of cloth with blood and fecal matter on it. The cloth was found to match a section of Catherine Eddowes's apron.

This meant that instead of fleeing deep into Whitechapel, the killer spent over an hour in the City in the vicinity of the Mitre

Square murder he had just committed. And presumably, he did this with blood on his hands and a section of blood-and fecal-stained cloth in his possession. He may even have wiped his bloody knife with the cloth.

The killer's actions appear to have been as follows: After murdering Eddowes, he fled from the City back into Whitechapel. But he proceeded no farther than a five-minute walk away, to Goulston Street. Thus, as the City Police were swarming to the scene of the just-committed murder in Mitre Square, the killer stayed close by for over an hour.

What was he doing during this time apart from, probably, wiping his hands and knife clean of blood? He had slipped unnoticed out of the City as that borough's police force began its pursuit of him and returned to Whitechapel, where the police had already been alerted to the Dutfield Yard murder forty-five minutes earlier. *And he left a calling card which brought both Metropolitan and City Police to the scene of the bloody apron in Goulston Street!*

Whatever explanation existed for the killer's actions and the police's inability to find him, by Sunday afternoon all of London seemed roused to action. The entire area between Berner Street and Mitre Square was packed with a constant stream of onlookers gripped by horrified curiosity. That same day, a mass gathering took place in Victoria Park, where a thousand people demanded that Home Secretary Henry Matthews and Metropolitan Police Commissioner Sir Charles Warren resign. Neither did, as least not yet.

For the moment, the reign of this cunning and reckless murderer was supreme.

CHAPTER 10

Metamorphosis

t had been thrilling in a way he had never experienced before. And on this morning after, he was more fulfilled than he would have thought possible.

How could that be? He had never been a violent man, or even an angry one. If he had believed as others did (which of course, he did not), he had sinned greatly and beyond redemption. He knew secretly that he had really *triumphed* greatly. But that wasn't it. He had a sense of *size*—as though he'd become much bigger than himself. That was absolutely true, of course. Still, it surprised him greatly.

He knew he should sleep, since he had been up all night. But that was impossible. He was exhilarated, filled with . . . *light*. Yes, it was precisely that: he was a being of light, not darkness.

His task was accomplished. He had accepted his burden and done his duty; and the result was a sense of satisfaction far beyond what he expected.

The truth was, he had been afraid. But not anymore.

Goodness, what a bundle of silly human emotions he was this morning! But that was all behind him now, wasn't it? And so he must stop thinking in those terms. He was . . . what? *Elevated* might be the right word. He was on a different plane now: one with the Other. This was sweet, and he wanted to enjoy his response—the human one—for just a little while longer.

But he knew he couldn't.

He was truly a man of his Age now—he represented the Age, all that was good and decent about it. For proof, he looked down at his hands. There will still some stains around the fingernails from the blood of the last woman—the second woman from last night— where the apron hadn't wiped it off. How he wished he could leave his hands just this way, and never wash away the stain of honor that was on them. Then, invisible, he could go back out on the streets, this time in the daylight, and watch the police in their frantic search for him.

And the people as well! He knew they'd be irresistibly drawn to the two places he'd been last night. They would be out today in the hundreds, perhaps thousands. He wanted to look in their eyes and see what they were really thinking as they gazed on the streets and the barricaded areas where the sacrifices had taken place.

He knew they agreed with him (though they couldn't admit it publicly)—that they were secretly glad about what he had done.

But none of that was possible. He had to disappear now, to go away and never come back. It was the price each of them had to pay, and the one they had all agreed to. Still, the change was worth it. He had shed his skin, going from the caterpillar to the butterfly. And now he was about to fly.

Did it matter that he had to leave London and watch the rest of it from afar?

This new creature—the new him—considered that thought. It shook its head, sadly, but happily too.

Goodness, but he was a bundle of new emotions this morning!

CHAPTER 11

The Laying On of Hands

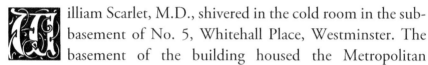illiam Scarlet, M.D., shivered in the cold room in the sub-basement of No. 5, Whitehall Place, Westminster. The basement of the building housed the Metropolitan Police's post-mortem facilities. Where Scarlet was standing now was one level lower still, in the sub-basement. This was the morgue, where a lift brought bodies up to the dissecting room one level above.

It was the coldest place in the building, the area where bodies could be kept uncorrupted for a surprising length of time. It didn't matter whether the bodies were intact or in pieces. Today, the latter was the case.

He was about to try something he had never attempted before, and he had no idea whether he would be successful. Yet he couldn't justify not trying it. He was here to lay his hands on the disassociated remains of the two men whose bodies had recently been found torn apart.

Gruesome though the task may be, Scarlet didn't think it was an unreasonable attempt. He had the power, unpredictable though it was, to see and participate in others' experiences—past and future—though objects and touch. Sometimes, it meant touching the person; or it might be merely an object the person had handled. The name for the phenomenon was *psychometry*, and Scarlet had been blessed or cursed with it from the time he was nine years old.

There was no reason, he was thinking now, why laying his hands on body parts should be different from touching those same bodies when they were intact. Whatever activated his occult sense must surely still be present in the pieces that had so recently been part of the whole.

This "gift" wasn't a skill he used lightly or regularly, especially since his boss, Chief Surgeon Sir Edward Mallinson, considered the practice to be akin to the dark arts. And of course, sometimes it didn't work at all. Often, what he saw and felt was quite accidental. He'd touch a person or an object that person had touched, and without any intention on his part, begin seeing a scene from their past or future. At other times—especially when an investigation was stymied or he was desperate—he'd intentionally try his luck.

As he was about to do right now.

The door to the morgue creaked as he closed it behind him, like something from a Gothic novel. He should use a little oil on it. Or something more slippery, like the adipose tissue around the heart of a fatted calf. He'd have to check what was best in *Dr. Scarlet's Book of Everyday Spells*. He smiled as he pictured Mallinson waving such a book over his head and shouting triumphantly: "*Look what I found in his foot locker!*"

The remains of the two dismembered men had been placed—as reverently as the morgue assistants could manage such a thing—into large galvanized tubs, the better to keep them cool in the basement. On three of these tubs, there was a white label tied to one of the handles on which a cramped hand had written: Haugen, Anders. This was the first of the male victims, who had been found in Green Dale Fields in Camberwell on September 3rd.

Nearby were three identical tubs with salmon-colored labels tied to their handles. On these, someone had used a thick-tipped carpenter's pencil to print in bold letters ROSS, GEORGE. This was the man found torn apart in the New Road in Whitechapel exactly a week after Anders Haugen's body was discovered.

To Scarlet, standing ten feet or so away, the contents of the tubs looked like pieces of a dressmaker's mannequin: arms, legs, head, and associated parts sitting ready for assembly. Except here, there were also pieces of faces, tufts of hair still rooted in a scalp, ears, eyeballs removed but still whole, and sections of internal organs— none of which, of course, would be found on a tailor's dress form. That, and stains, streaks, and splashes of rusty red which covered everything in the tubs.

Either Scarlet could dwell on what he was seeing or carry out what he came here to do. Without thinking any further on what was before him, he locked the door, removed and hung up his coat, and rolled up his sleeves.

He knelt before the tub labeled Haugen, Anders. Deciding that it would be too much like a comic opera to pick up an arm and examine it closely as if it were a turkey drumstick, he closed his eyes and reached downward. The palm of his left hand touched cold flesh; that of his right hand, a section of rough cloth, like that of a jacket or coat. He silently prayed that something would come—that he wouldn't have to root around in the cold human stew before him until a remnant from the last moments of this man arose inside *him*, lighting up his brain.

Something did come.

It jolted Scarlet and nauseated him. And of course, he was trapped inside it and couldn't look away or escape the horror of the thing. It was happening to him exactly as it had to Anders Haugen, three weeks ago in London's Green Dale Fields, in the man's last moments on earth . . .

I need time to think.
That's exactly what you don't have, Anders. And you know it.
I have to leave soon—very soon. That's the ironclad rule, and I can't

break it. What is breaking my heart is Ingunn, that I have to leave her behind. It will only be for a short while; I'll send for her. All the same, she can't know I'm leaving. That would be too risky.

It's a warm evening. I don't need this jacket. It's lightweight, though, so I'll keep it on.

Funny how the mind shies away from dealing with a hard decision! Here I am thinking about the weather. That was some cold in July when it snowed up north, wasn't it? Snow in July—and this is England, not Norway! Tonight is pleasant, though. There's the Dylways Road up ahead . . . I can cut over to the fields from here.

Peckman Road is a good place to live, with Ruskin Park and Green Dale Fields so close by. It's nice to unwind with a walk like this after a day of loadin' and unloadin' them wagons. The fresh air is good too. There won't be any shortage of work coming up, as far as I can see. We're haulin' more than ever. Old Man Baldroy must be happy. . . . Well, what passes as happy for him, the grim sonofabitch. Ha!

Which path? — The left one today, the one with the wooden bench. There are the lads playing football down below on the pitch. Uh: I couldn't run like that now if you paid me. Not at my weight, never mind me legs! Ingunn jokes that I'm twice the man I was when she married me, the saucy wench!

Ingunn.

Ah, shit. I need to stop, and go back to that bench. Need to sit and think. What's wrong with me, blabbin' on in my mind about this and that nothing? I need to think things through.

How will she take it? I can't tell her I'm off—I'll just have to leave a note. But it has to be soon. It's already been two days now since the deed. I'll have to be gone by Wednesday morning at the latest, the day after next. I should have planned better. The railways to the west is my ticket—that's what it will have to be. Even the others can't know where I'm goin', that's another of the rules.

Well, the task—my duty—is done now. Can't change it. Everything will be all right, Haugen. Everything will be all right.

What's that up ahead? Them's those gardens, set out in sections separated by planks or bricks and stone. I think they call 'em raised gardens. Never noticed them much before. Why now? Did I see something moving there a minute ago? I'll go closer now to take a look. Å, min, it's thick in here. Like a jungle, with all these vegetables and flowers still bloomin' in early September. . . .

There. Something's movin' to the right, behind that wall of plants and climbin' vines on that wire structure. Gettin' dark, and I can't see past those fucking giant chard plants. There it is again—now it's moving back to the left. I see it now.

Oh, Jesus. That's a lion. *What's a lion doing here? What the fuck— a lion strolling through a garden in Camberwell? Christ.* Don't move. *Did it see me? Should I shout, or run? No, that's a terrible idea. Lions run after prey. I don't want to become prey.*

Can't see anything through all that foliage. Wait. Oh, shit. There it is—like a giant cat, crouching behind those vines, watching me.

It's getting up slowly, taking its time, coming out from behind its cover, still watching me. Å, Gud. Å, Gud! There's two more, movin' toward me the same way. Walking slowly, crouching low to the ground now, all their eyes on me.

*Å stå med skjegget i postkassen.**
I feel cold, and numb.

Now Scarlet was experiencing other thoughts. He didn't 'hear' them, for they didn't appear to be coming from Anders Haugen.

He suddenly knew that these were Nemean lions, from the Peloponnese in Greece—and they were creatures with supernatural powers. They had golden fur and claws that were longer and sharper than other lions and they couldn't be killed with mortal weapons.

He also knew that Anders Haugen, freight-wagon loader, had no idea why they had come for him. But the Norwegian labourer realized what they were about to do to him. He had time to say a

---

* Colloquial Norwegian expression: "I'm standing with my beard in the mailbox." Or, "I'm in trouble now."

mad thought to himself in Norwegian. It had to be inspired by the lion's golden fur, and their cat-like smiles, and his own savage fate.

Morgenstund har gull I munn. 'Morning time is gold in the mouth,' or in English, the early bird catches the worm.

He screamed *"NEI!"* just once.

Scarlet also experienced everything that happened next—in the terrible thirty seconds or so while the man whose remains he was touching had still been conscious and feeling.

Then he vomited on the morgue floor.

CHAPTER 12

A Woman of the Future

She was as proud of her room as if she'd landed in a pot of jam. Her own room! Never mind that the courtyard wasn't nothing to write home about. Getting the privacy of a room where she could take her customers was still a stroke of luck, and no bloody doubt about it.

To be sure, the place was tiny. It was really an afterthought, as the larger space next door at No. 26 had been walled off to create this separate living area. Miller's Court was as poor as anyplace in Spitalfields, at the end of a narrow dark passageway from Dorset Street through an arched doorway that looked like the entrance to a tomb. But her place, No. 13, Miller's Court, was a *room*—her own room (she couldn't help repeating that thought in her head), not a lodging house bed.

It was small: 10 feet by 12 feet or so, and filled up with a bed, a fireplace, a small table to eat at, a chest for dishes, and a smaller table near the bed. And, of course, she shared it with her man, when he bothered to be around. It did take the egg, though. Listen . . . it was a damn sight better than lifting your skirts against a wall every night to scare up enough money for a bed in a doss house.

She didn't mind that those who lived in the tenement houses overlooking the Court could look down from their second-floor windows and see her room. No. 13 was the first place you came to after you walked through the passageway and into the courtyard: the first room on the right after the "tomb" entrance.

On the wall of her place around the corner from the front (and only) door were two windows. She'd put up a curtain on the larger window, and hung up an old coat over the other one to maintain privacy. That window, the smaller one near the door, had two panes of broken glass out of the four—the result of an argument with Joe Barnett, her man. He was out of work and she was £1 9s behind in her rent; but the landlord, Mr. McCarthy, was a good enough sort and he didn't press her too hard about it. As far as she was concerned—and all things considered, dearie—she was absolutely in a pot of jam.

Besides, she was tall and young and attractive, never mind that she was a bit stout. One bloke—the cocky devil—had called her "All very fine and large," which she believed was the refrain of a song. It was true, though. Her ample figure, along with her youth (she was only 22), and even her Irish accent for some of her customers, meant that she never lacked for clients. Joe could go his own merry way and she knew she'd be all right.

Her name was Mary Jane Kelly, and like so many other unfortunates in the East End in 1888, she was one woman when sober, another when drunk. She was a singer of Irish songs (whether sober or inebriated), and kind enough to invite fellow prostitutes into her small room when they were homeless. She seemed to be on good terms with her neighbors in Miller's Court, though she didn't have many friends. "She was one of the most decent and nice girls you could meet when sober," said one acquaintance, but became "very quarrelsome and abusive" when she'd been drinking.

As with everyone in London at this time, the murders and mutilations of East End street-walkers had touched Mary Jane Kelly. In Dorset Street, for instance, not more than a few feet from the entrance to Miller's Court, a bill announcing the *Illustrated Police News* £100 reward for information on the killer was posted on a wall. And Mary Jane seemed to have a fascination with the case, for several times she had asked Barnett to read the newspapers stories about the killings aloud to her.

On the other hand, a month had gone by since the last murders: the double event in the early morning of 30 September. It was easy to let the more pressing affairs of every day take one's mind away from it all. There was the money for the back rent to think about, for one thing; or more immediately, where the coins would come from for her next drink.

The Ripper murders could go on without her.

CHAPTER 13

Retribution

has Widdington sat on the bed in his shabby furnished room on Wollaston Close in London's Elephant and Castle section in Southwark, wondering whether the hands of the clock on his kitchen table had stopped.

It would take twenty-three minutes, he knew, for the horse-drawn omnibus to take him from the Close to Liverpool Street. The first train to Witham on the Great Eastern Railway line left from Liverpool Street Station at 04.23, and he aimed to be on it. It was now 3.10 a.m. He had planned to give himself an hour for the bus ride, for safety's sake, and leave at 3.20 or so; but he could see now that he wasn't going to be able to keep that schedule. But he still had enough time.

The problem was the *clock*. He was sure that at least two or three minutes had gone by as he sat here staring at it. Yet it still said 3.10!

Obviously, he thought, it's stopped. He looked down at his shoes (he was already dressed), wondering how he was possibly going to know when he *really* had to leave, for he didn't own a pocket watch. When he looked up at the clock again, it read 3:14 . . . so four minutes had gone by after all.

He smiled at his trepidation over this little affair of the clock. No one was playing tricks with him. It was just another example of how there were powers far beyond the everyday directing events now.

It was part and parcel with his feeling that he was involved with something *larger* now. It was the very same feeling he'd had then . . . the morning nearly a month ago that he'd killed the two women—one in Dutfield Yard and the other in Mitre Square—and when he had felt like he was a bundle of new emotions.

He realized now that events were pre-ordained. Even the railroad he would be taking this morning—The Great Eastern Railway Line—and the new station he'd be leaving from(!) seemed propitious. He had made his decision, and was now headed into the "Great East" himself.

It was true that it was only the town of Witham in Essex, the county to the east of London, that he was going to, and not anywhere exotic. But somehow it was fitting. And Liverpool Street Station, where the train would depart from, was somewhat new as well. It was only fourteen years old, having replaced Bishopsgate station which, Mr. Widdington knew from living in the area all his life, had been in the same part of London, though on Shoreditch High Street.

He was heading eastward, starting a new life, *and* he'd be leaving from a newly-built railway station. Yes, 'propitious' was the word!

He had done a terrible yet great thing, and now he had to hightail it away from here to save his skin. There was no sense in hiding his head in the clouds and denying that there were practical details to consider. But he had fiddled and fiddled, and now a month had passed and he still hadn't left London. He had been careful, though—he was reasonably certain none of the others had seen him. But now he was truly leaving.

He was a small man, but ever since that night and morning of the 29th-30th of September, he had felt *different*. It was true that his mind was still somewhat in turmoil. But at last he was setting out on a path . . . *his* path. There was no turning back now. Somehow, the magnitude of that thought comforted him.

All his life, Mr. Widdington had known that he was meant for something special. But the magnitude of *this* act he had committed and its aftermath made his head spin. How could any human being have known that he would be singled out for such a role? Let the people all around him—the 'great unwashed,' as Bulwer-Lytton had it—worship their false gods of money, middle-class comfort, their weak and powerless religions, and most hypocritically, the pleasures of the flesh. It was an honor to shake the foundations of their beliefs through the thing he'd been asked to do, and had carried out! He and his brothers in faith were bringing glory to the Empire, even if the fools they were helping didn't realize it.

The work was dangerous, though, so dangerous.

And so he must leave. Did it matter that no one would ever know his name and the part he had played in saving society? No. And anyway, that wasn't any different from what his life had been up to now, was it? He had always been invisible, working in the restaurant and library of a gentlemen's club. That he could do both jobs was because he was an educated man. He wasn't even given credit for that however, since he hadn't attended an exclusive "public" school or elite university.

But the club he worked at was among the most renowned in London! It was the United Service Club, at 116 *Pall Mall*, the street famous for its clubs. United Service was one of the most exclusive, too: well known for allowing only those above the rank of Major in the British Army or Commander in the Royal Navy to join it. And in this too he was lucky. Many of the clubs—and especially those with military memberships—hired non-commissioned officers for its staff, men who were retiring from their service and were recommended by their senior officers who were members of the club. He himself had never served in the military. Of course, he knew deep down that it wasn't luck—it was ability and brains that got him the position. But no one ever really saw the true extent of his abilities and the range of his mind.

Suddenly, Mr. Widdington chuckled aloud at the paradox his thinking had just uncovered for him. All of London now knew what he had done—was ablaze with it, in fact—but he'd never get any credit for it. He was equally invisible and famous. His deed was on everyone's lips, but no one had the remotest idea that it was he who had accomplished it. He considered this for a moment until, suddenly, it didn't seem such an amusing thought anymore.

He emerged from this reverie and glanced automatically at the clock. It read 3.35. Mr. Widdington, unknown hero of his age, began scrambling to put the last few items in his second-hand Gladstone bag and head down the stairs.

He soon discovered that it wasn't only workers in the fish and food markets that had to get to work early. The bus was crowded even at this hour. Liverpool Street Station, however, was another thing entirely. Few people seemed inclined to hop on a railways train heading off to distant parts at four o'clock in the morning.

There, on the West Side No. 1 platform, sat the train: a lazy stream of white smoke drifting upward out of the locomotive's stack. The train looked to Mr. Widdington like an iron monster dozing until it was time to awaken and start on its journey. There weren't more than a half-dozen people walking toward it on the platform. The clock mounted on the roof of the Abercorn Books stall in the vast lobby told him that he had eighteen minutes to spare.

He began walking down the steep two-tiered stairway to the track level, and had reached the first landing when he heard his name called. Incongruously (he thought), the voice was soft, but he heard it clearly over the noise of the station all around him.

"Chas. Chas."

Whoever was calling him obviously knew him, since nearly everyone else made the mistake of thinking that his first name was the written abbreviation of 'Charles'. He thought the voice was coming from someplace below him. That didn't make sense, because he saw only some storage rooms down there beside the train's platform. So, he turned around and looked back *up* the stairway, to the main concourse above him. There were only two men and a boy up there, the three of them leaning on the railing and looking at the train, not at him.

"Chas!"

More insistent this time. And it *was* coming from below. His heart sped up as he realized what someone calling his name meant. It had to be one of the others from the group, here because it was known that he was leaving town by this train. But how would they have known? And were they here to bid him goodbye, to chastise him, or something worse? Were they angry that he'd taken a month to finally go, when he should have done it a day or two after the deed?

By now, he'd reached the bottom of the stairway. He stood there and stared into the darkness of the three large open spaces in front of him. From here, all three resembled caves as much as they did storage spaces, which is what they probably were. They all had high arched entranceways in the architectural style of the station, without any doors, and they were dark because there were no lights burning in the interior of any of them. The two to the left looked empty, while the one on the right seemed filled with building supplies set down haphazardly inside.

"Over here!"

It was clear from this close that the voice was coming from the middle space, the one nearest the stairs. He actually had to duck under the staircase to reach it.

Wisely, as he thought, he stopped at the entrance, not entering the darkened area.

"Who is it? Who's there?"

There was no response. He heard something, a shuffling sound, or perhaps something sliding along the floor. He imagined whoever was in there sliding a board or other obstruction aside in order to come out to meet him, or to allow him to go inside. But no one came out.

For a moment, he thought of turning around and running for the nearest steps leading up into the train. He didn't have much time before the train left, after all! But he realized that would be a stupid act on his part. If it looked like he was running away, it would go badly for him with the others. He took a few small, tentative steps into the dark space.

"Who's in there?" he said insistently. He'd meant to sound put out, inconvenienced, even angry, but he knew he hadn't succeeded. He was about halfway in—he actually stopped with his right leg bent, ready to swing forward—when he saw something *slither* in the darkness to his right.

Whatever it was, the thing was huge—maybe a dozen feet long and two feet high—and somehow blacker than the blackness around it. He grew frozen with fear. Then, he saw the same thing to his left, and another move across the dark space directly in front of him. Whatever it was, there were *three* of them.

At the same time, in a way that was perfectly synchronized, the three slithering shapes pivoted so that they were facing him.

And once again, Mr. Widdington was lucky. For these were basilisks, giant snakes or serpents, and to look into their eyes meant instant death. Mr. Widdington had looked, so he was already dead on the floor of the storage space when three sets of razor-sharp teeth, all of the same shape and cutting excellence, began to sink in and tear, sink in and tear, again and again.

CHAPTER 14

A Sharp Observation

On the next-to-last day in October, the giant boilers of London's Liverpool Street Station were fired up for the season, making the entire building stiflingly hot. So it only took thirty-six hours for the body in the catacombs underneath the main concourse to be discovered. Or, to be accurate, the *pieces* of a body scattered throughout the storage area underneath the stairway leading to the West Side No. 1 track.

The unfortunate discoverer was a lad of seventeen named Edward Leggett. Leggett was a coal-porter who had been tasked with fetching a wheelbarrow from one of the cave-like storage spaces near the track. By that time, however, the stench had spread outward and upward, giving nearly everyone walking on the concourse above the unmistakable facial expression that indicates a bad smell.

Eddie had no trouble recognizing by the light of his lantern that the body parts spread out before him were human. Which is why he reported it immediately to his foreman, who passed on the news to the Railways office, which promptly notified the Metropolitan Police.

Two hours later, the remains were at Scotland Yard's headquarters at No. 5, Whitehall Place. Prudence, however, had kept the foul-smelling evidence out of the post-mortem area in the basement. Instead, the body parts were placed in three tubs set outside in the fresh air in a nonpublic courtyard between buildings

Nos. 4 and 5, which is where Dr. William Scarlet was currently examining them.

Scarlet had volunteered for the task. In truth, there wasn't a stampede among the assistant police surgeons on duty to examine the remains. But he had a good reason to be here. One fact was inescapable: the *outré* nature of the killings of the two men he'd already examined, with their savage dismemberment, indicated a strong possibility of a supernatural cause in all of the cases.

Two pieces of evidence supported that view: the nature of the wounds themselves, and the curious vision he'd seen when touching the remains of Anders Haugen. If there was another explanation for lions from a legend to be stalking a man in London's Green Dale Gardens, he was more than ready to hear it.

His initial foray into examining the remains of the two male victims had yielded only the clues that Haugen's body parts had offered. He'd also placed his hands in the tubs of the second victim, George Ross. But as often happened, his psychometric ability had yielded nothing—he didn't see or feel anything that Ross had experienced before his death.

It was time to try now with the remains of this man, who had just been discovered in the catacombs under Liverpool Street Station.

A torn-apart wallet and a train reservation on his person had identified him as Chas Widdington, an employee of the United Service Club in Pall Mall. Now Scarlet was ready to try—for the third time—to see if anything from the scattered remnants of the man's death could reveal anything about his life.

A cravat soaked in cologne covered Scarlet's mouth and nose, held in place by an old winter scarf tied at the back of his neck. He opted not to wear gloves, as that would disrupt his physical contact with the corpse. He'd simply have to put up with the putrescent nature of the remains.

He stepped up to one of the three tubs containing the now-rotting body parts of Mr. Widdington and went down on his knees. Fortunately, the windows above him in both buildings were covered with grime. If anyone was looking down at him at the moment, they would see a police surgeon examining a corpse found in a public place. He, and they, would have to let it go at that.

He believed that he and Pierce-Jones had an advantage over anyone else at the Yard who was investigating this death and that of the two other men. The Metropolitan Police had enough experts on hand to have already recognized that all three of the cases indicated an animal attack. But conventional thinking would only allow them an unimaginative conclusion: that a creature or creatures was on the loose from a circus or zoo, and these men had been unfortunate enough to have become their prey. The fact that no such escaped animals had been found had stymied the Yard's efforts at further investigation. And of course, the public and newspaper frenzy over the East End murders of four prostitutes—by a monster everyone was now calling Jack the Ripper—had greatly distracted the Yard's focus on anything else that was going on in the city.

All of which were helping keep Scarlet's private sleuthing unnoticed.

The container he was kneeling at offered small pieces of remains on top. Uppermost was a portion of Widdington's right hand: the thumb, forefinger, and middle finger—all still intact—and two small bones, the scaphoid and lunate. It seemed as good a place as any to start. And so Scarlet placed his own right hand on the cold partial hand in front of him.

But once again he was disappointed. Nothing came. He moved to the other two tubs in turn, touching a variety of parts or holding in his hand pieces as small as a thumbnail. But he felt nothing—no vision arose in his own mind of this man's last moments—and he replaced the covers on the containers.

Suddenly, a thought of a very different nature came to him.

Before it had formed fully in his mind, he was stripping off the scarf and cologne-scented cravat and leaving the courtyard. He was on his way to the outside world and his friend Pierce-Jones.

"What if they're related?"

Django, who was tapping the hard-boiled egg in front of him with a spoon, looked up from his breakfast table.

"Well, happy All Hallows' Eve to you, too," he said, "even if it's just morning." He smiled. "Which reminds me: why are you breaking into my house at this time of the day and disturbing my breakfast?"

"Hardly breaking in," protested Scarlet, looking down at Django's breakfast and realizing he was hungry. Before he could ask about remedying that situation, however, his host was gesturing to his man Wilfred and pointing to a vacant place at the table.

Tap-tap-tap-tap-tap. This was followed by some delicate surgery focused on removing parts of the egg shell.

"What if *what* are related?" asked Django, intent on the operation he was performing.

"The prostitutes' murders and those of the three men."

That stopped the egg surgery.

"How so?"

"The timing," answered Scarlet. "The modus operandi are wildly different, of course. And I don't see how the animal attacks on the men are related to the slit throats and disemboweling of the women. But, see here," and he placed the advertising calendar he'd brought with him on the table.

At that moment, Wilfred brought Scarlet's serving of his own hard-boiled egg, bacon, poached haddock, toast, and a sliced Thomas Rivers apple. Django had already poured out tea at Scarlet's place at the table.

"Look at the dates," said the physician, eating and pointing at dates on the calendar at the same time. "Our first victim of the Whitechapel Murderer—or Jack the Ripper or whatever you want to call him—was Mary Ann Nichols, on August thirty-first. Anders Haugen, the first of the men who were found torn apart, was killed three days later, on the third of September. You remember . . . you came late to the Society's meeting that night and told everyone."

He went on before Pierce-Jones could reply.

"The second of the prostitutes' killings was of Annie Chapman, who was found in Hanbury Street on the morning of the eighth of September. George Ross, the second of the male victims, was killed *two days later*, on September 10th. Then, we have the double-murder on the last day of September: Elizabeth Stride at around 1.00 a.m. in Dutfield Yard, and just forty-five minutes later, Catherine Eddowes in Mitre Square in the City."

Now Django interrupted.

"But Chas Widdington—whose remains you just examined, and I'm eager to hear what you found out, by the way—was just discovered yesterday. Given the state of the body as I understand it, he was probably killed a day or two earlier, on October twenty-eighth or twenty-ninth. Do you agree?"

"Yes, I'm sure you're right," allowed Scarlet.

"Well, that's an entire month after the previous two female victims, who were murdered on the same night of September 30th. If Widdington's death is linked to those two murders, how do you account for the sudden gap?"

"I have no idea. Yet."

"And how are all these killings related? Is the person—or persons—who is stalking women in the East End also going after these men?"

"Presumably," replied Scarlet.

"By why the wildly different method of killing the women versus the men? And what do the men have in common with the women? Were they customers, or procurers?"

Scarlet concentrated on his breakfast for a long moment. Then he sighed and shook his head slightly.

"I asked when I came in, what if the murders are related?" he reminded his friend. "I didn't say I had any answers yet."

"Sorry," said Django. "I was thinking out loud more than anything." He waited a few seconds. "What about this morning? Did you get anything from, well, . . . that is, touching the remains?"

Scarlet seemed dismissive of the matter and intent on something else. As indeed, he was.

"No, nothing. But all of this gives me another idea."

"What's that, old man?"

"I need to take a closer look at the photographs of the dead women," came the reply.

Scarlet was tired from his early-morning foray to the forensic lab at No. 5, Whitehall Place to examine Chas Widdington's remains, and had intended to go home afterwards to get some sleep. But now he was in the building again, this time in his office. On his desk was a thin stack of all the photos taken of the four female victims of the Whitechapel Murderer/Jack the Ripper.

He spread the photos out on the desktop, arranging them from left to right in chronological order: Mary Ann Nichols, Annie Chapman, Elizabeth Stride, Catherine Eddowes. These were the only crime scene photographs taken of the victims, which he had access to from the case files.

Three of the seven photos in front of him were useless for his needs: those of Nichols, Chapman, and Stride. He wasn't sure why post-mortem photos hadn't been taken immediately of these women, but that was the case.

The first of the murdered prostitutes, Mary Ann Nichols, had been photographed in her coffin, wearing a white dress that was buttoned up to her neck. Only one of the two neck incisions was visible, and only in its upper edge. Scarlet knew that the woman had abdominal wounds as well, both vertical and horizontal, but there was no chance for him now to look at them.

Annie Chapman's photo was even worse. Her head and torso down to the sternum were shown, but she too was fully dressed. In her case, the high neckline of the dress she'd been posed in completely obscured the neck incisions that, as with all the Whitechapel victims, had killed her.

Elizabeth Stride's photo was better: there was no collar to the dress she'd been posed in, and he could see the right half of the throat incision (the rest of the wound was in shadow). Scarlet lingered over this photo with his magnifying glass. But this effort also proved to be unproductive: the throat wound had been closed before the photograph was taken.

The four Catherine Eddowes photos, on the other hand, were outstanding for his purpose. These were true post-mortem photos of a naked victim. There were two head-shots, one head-and-torso down to approximately the lowest rib, and one in which the victim had been propped against a wall as if standing and a full-length photograph taken.

The facial wounds on Eddowes as compared to the three previous women—none of whom had been mutilated facially—were frightful. As Scarlet knew from the autopsy report, following the standard throat incision that had killed her, Catherine Eddowes's face had been extensively mutilated, including seventeen different cuts and the excision of the tip of the nose. The gash in the throat was particularly extensive and savage, extending for six or seven inches and reaching as deep as the intervertebral cartilages. Scarlet lingered long over each of the facial wounds with the magnifying glass.

Next, he examined the abdominal and pubic wounds Catherine Eddowes had sustained after death. These wounds were also extensive. Eddowes's abdomen had been sliced open all the way from the breast bone to the pubes, involving both her vagina and rectum. The liver had been stabbed, and the left kidney removed. Dr. Brown, the doctor who performed the autopsy, felt that the killer had kneeled on the right side of the dead woman slightly below the middle of the body as he did his work.

Scarlet had no opinion on this. At any rate, it was impossible to tell from the photographs whether that was what had happened, for the best image concerning the abdominal wounds was the one posing Eddowes in a standing position.

Another frustrating aspect of the photographic evidence was the fact that the post-mortem had been concluded and the autopsy incisions stitched up before the standing photo was taken. There was one gross incision, however, that Scarlet believed was not part of opening up the body during autopsy. That was what he was looking at now through the magnifying glass.

From what he was seeing, this cut was from the killer, not the dissecting doctor.

This cut—the main deep incision carried out immediately after death—was of an unusual shape. It procceded straight downward from the sternum to the navel. But then it swerved sharply to the right for five inches; from there, it continued in a vertical direction again until it reached the vagina.

Why the sudden and abrupt change of direction?

Now he bent forward, placing the magnifying glass as close to the photo as he could without causing distortion. He moved the glass slowly and painstakingly over the entirety of this wound, back and forth a number of times.

Then he sat up straight and considered what he had seen.

A wave of exhaustion was overtaking him now, and he knew he had to get home and to bed. He could visit the cutlery shops when he woke up. Better yet, he'd do it in the morning, when he would be fresh.

CHAPTER 15

All Hallows' Eve

onight was October 31st—All Hallows' Eve—and they all felt the significance of the date.

They didn't care whether this date was originally connected with a Celtic harvest festival or the Christian church's night before All Saints Day. The Celts and the Christians both were newcomers compared to the gods they worshipped. Yet they too felt the mystery of the changing year and the beginning of the months of darkness.

They were the Friends of the Daughters of Night. They worshipped the Moirai or Fates, who had ruled over the lives of men and women for nearly four thousand years.

There were three Fates. *Clotho* was the Spinner who spun the thread of life. *Lachesis*, the Drawer of Lots, measured the length of each life. And, most important for the Friends, there was *Atropos*, the Unyielding, who cut the thread at the appointed time without pity or sympathy.

But Atropos had commanded them the last time they summoned her from beneath the earth in the Chislehurst Caves not to do so again. In fact, they were not to gather together any more. From now on, only the one chosen each time would return to the Caves to get the instrument which had been left there by the one before him.

They had heard Atropos speak, and they obeyed.

Still, each in his own way thought of the ancient ceremonies that had taken place on All Hallows' Eves before now, and of the long winter nights to come. But most of all, they remembered their devotion to the dark worship of the Fates.

And of the duty which these gods had assigned to them.

CHAPTER 16

Scarlet Goes A-Hunting

The cutlery shops of London were mostly gathered in a section off Waterloo Road on the South Bank called, appropriately enough, The Cut. The street was well known for this particular commodity, the same way that Thames Street was famous for its cheeses, Covent Garden for its fruits, and Monmouth Street for second-hand clothing.

Scarlet was quite clear in his mind what he was looking for, at the same time that he had no idea what it would look like when he found it. He would be quite dependent on the expertise of the merchants in The Cut for the latter, which was precisely why he had come south of the river. He wished he could have brought the Eddowes photos with him to explain what he was looking for, but of course that was out of the question.

The first shop he was attracted to, like a moth to a flame, was named Coutellerie, French for "Cutlery." It had an irresistible display of wares in its window, with three tiers of instruments set out neatly on shelves of glass. There were pocket-knives: hundreds of these, with all types of handles from polished wood to exquisitely carved bone. Next in abundance were men's razors, along with badger-hair brushes to use with them. An entire shelf of scissors of all sizes and functions was displayed above that, singly and in sets ensconced in velvet cases. At the sides of the great display window were sets of carving and steak knives for the table. The top shelf displayed surgical instruments, and what Scarlet could only term curiosities that contained one or more cutting surfaces.

Surely, he thought, whoever owned this store must know everything about knives and would be able to answer his question. But he was immediately disappointed. The owner or manager's French accent was amateurly done, and the man became vastly uninterested once he decided a sale wasn't forthcoming. That assumption was wrong, but Scarlet wasn't about to tell him that. The fake monsieur was also completely unimpressed by his visitor's Scotland Yard credential. Scarlet vowed not to make that mistake again.

The next shop, Brent Bros. Cutlery, was manned by the owner's young son of perhaps fourteen or fifteen, who was handling the store while his father was out delivering an order. The boy had no trade knowledge whatsoever, and Scarlet didn't spend any time there.

He should have known from the name of the third establishment he tried that they wouldn't be able to help him either. London Cutlery and Serveware specialized in instruments designed for fine dining: caddy spoons for measuring tea portions, asparagus servers, knife rests, snail forks, sugar nips, marrow scoops and the like, most of the delicate items made of pewter or silver.

The fourth shop was named simply The Cut. Looking at the small sign above the front door, Scarlet decided he liked the simplicity of naming one's business after the neighborhood famous for its cutlery.

The old gent behind the counter might have been there when the building was erected. Scarlet decided the fellow might have been wearing the same style of outfit since then as well. He wore an old-fashioned cutaway coat, a starched white shirt with black tie, and a bowler hat pushed back on his head, accentuating his bushy head of white hair and carefully trimmed beard of the same color. He looked up from his task of applying the edge of a knife to the grinder which sat on the long shelf he was standing behind. He had been humming, but stopped the instant he noticed Scarlet approaching the counter.

"'morning, sir," he offered. Then he looked back down and gave the grinder one last spin. "Mm-hm," he said, angling the knife he was holding to the light.

"Filet knife," he announced, holding it up for Scarlet's inspection. "Need to be careful with these. The blade is so long and thin, before you know it you'll be grinding nothing." He laughed. "How can I help you, sir?"

"Well, honestly, I'm not sure you can," came the answer. 'My name is Dr. William Scarlet," he said, offering his hand.

"Hiram Joseph," said the proprietor. He quickly wiped his own hand on a cloth on the counter and grasped Scarlet's hand in a grip of steel. Then he slid the filet knife back into its slot on a block that rested on a shelf behind him, and gave his customer his full attention.

"I'm interested in a cutting instrument," Scarlet began. He realized immediately it was an obvious and foolish way to begin with a knife merchant. But Hiram Joseph continued to look at him attentively.

"I'm a surgeon, and this concerns an abdominal incision. Well, the truth is, a patient suffered a serious wound in an attack, and I'm trying to find the instrument that might have done it." He avoided mentioning that this was a murder case—and above all that his inquiry had anything to do with the Whitechapel killings.

"The general opinion is that a sharp, long-bladed knife was used," Scarlet went on. "But it seems to me that the incision was thicker in width than that. And whatever was used has a beveled surface on both sides, not just one side like a knife. Also . . . and I know this doesn't make any sense, the *length* of the blade seemed to change—from a sharp point at the beginning of the incision, to *two* sharp points with a considerable space between them as the incision continued downward for three and a half inches."

He wondered whether that was too much information to hand the cutler all at once. But Mr. Joseph simply nodded, and asked a question that surprised Scarlet.

"Was there any mark on the skin of a round protuberance, like the head of a screw or a nut?"

"Not that I could see," Scarlet answered. He didn't want to mention that his observations had come from examining a photograph, not the body itself.

The other man nodded again, then disappeared into a room behind the counter. When he returned, he lifted Scarlet's right hand and placed something heavy in it.

Scarlet looked down at what he was holding.

"Scissors?"

"Not scissors, Doctor," replied Mr. Joseph. "Shears." He pointed to the tool. "You'll notice the weight and the thickness of the blades, sir. They're meant for heavier work than scissors. Also," and he took the shears back and turned them over, "you can see that both blades are beveled. You could stab with these, or open the blades and make an incision—even in the same cut, if you use both hands."

It seemed a perfect solution to Scarlet—an almost elegant one, in fact. But he said:

"Why did you ask about a round mark?"

The tradesman pointed to the center of the tool. "Here's the hinge, held together with a screw and nut. All shears have that, just like scissors, so the two blades can move separately. But look here," and he took out a pad from an inside pocket of his coat and the stub of a carpenter's pencil from his trousers pocket. Then he began drawing a shape on the pad. The shape was unmistakable as shears, yet it was of a primitive design that was hardly like modern shears at all.

"I don't know if this has any bearing on the cutting tool you're looking for," Joseph said as he drew, "but this would solve the fact that there wasn't a hinge mark in the flesh. Take a look at this."

The finished drawing was instantly recognizable as a primitive yet ingenious example of shears. In the drawing, the modern design of two separate blades (each with handles including holes for the fingers) wasn't in evidence. Instead, the entire tool was forged from a single piece of metal. The top blade—as sharp and tapered as a modern one—narrowed at its base to become a handle which then curved, unbroken, around at the back, so that the shape could repeat itself in the opposite direction, ending with an identical bottom blade. The blades were skillfully honed and angled so they would act as cutting edges when pressed downward just as with modern shears. But in the ancient design, the open space between the base of the blades was where the pressure of the user's hand was applied with, presumably, a squeezing motion. It was a simple and completely functional design that used only one piece of forged metal, with no hinge necessary.

Scarlet gathered that this must be an ancient design that existed before the modern version with separate hinged blades evolved. But it looked just as sharp, and was probably as efficient as the modern equivalent in its cutting and shearing actions.

Scarlet stared down at the drawing, the look on his face somber. This was not just a lesson in archeology. The shears he was looking at might have been used in a series of recent murders.

"When were tools like this made?" he asked.

"The shears you're looking at, sir, were invented in Ancient Egypt," Hiram Joseph answered. "Around 1,500 B.C. or so. The hinged version we're familiar with was first used by the Romans around 100 A.D. So, if you were looking for shears like the one on that pad, they would have been in use sometime between those two periods."

"How do you know this?"

"Oh, ancient tool design is a hobby of mine . . . connected with my trade, of course."

"But if someone wanted to use something like what you've drawn, could it be made nowadays?"

"Of course. Any good blacksmith could make something similar to that design."

"Where would I look for someone like that?" asked Scarlet.

But Mr. Joseph shook his head.

"I wouldn't bother, my friend," he said. "If someone in London had been commissioned to forge an instrument like that, I would have heard about it. You'd be much better off looking for an original . . . maybe in a museum, someplace like that."

"You're serious?"

"Dead serious," replied the cutler.

CHAPTER 17

Horace Bilby

t is said that the good reader makes the good book. If that is true, then presumably, a good historian can make the world as it existed before the present time. And following this line of reasoning, the truly remarkable reader will uncover the past as it existed and tell it to us in his own "good book." But where would you find such an exceptional reader?

You would ask for Horace Bilby, if you knew about him—which you wouldn't. William Scarlet and Django Pierce-Jones knew, however. And they were perfectly happy to settle for an in-depth report in lieu of an actual book.

Their nickname for him was, in fact, "The Reader."

Horace Bilby was a researcher par excellence, and that was what made him dangerous. He was a little man of fifty or seventy—you couldn't tell which—with a balding head fringed with soft white hair that somehow reminded one of a rabbit. He habitually wore a coat of rusty black which was at least twenty years out of date. Bilby cared not a whit (which is probably how he would put it) about his appearance, however.

Horace Bilby cared about research.

It would not be going too far to say that reading was everything to Bilby. In fact, if he had emerged from the womb without a volume of *Land Holdings of the English Gentry, 1509 to the Present* in his tiny hand, Scarlet would have been amazed to hear it. He ran a private concern offering the most discreet and in-depth research services of records of all kinds. So private and circumspect was the firm, in fact, that it had no name. Anything that had ever been recorded, catalogued, or filed somewhere in the British Isles, however obscure the record might be, was the domain of The Reader and his small staff. Scarlet used him regularly. Each time, he was eternally grateful that Bilby's nameless firm was unknown outside of the *demimonde* of the governmental, commercial, and criminal worlds of London.

On this occasion, however—and it was fairly maddening to him—Scarlet had no firm direction to point Bilby in. He had discussed the recent events at length with Pierce-Jones, in fact, in an attempt to *gain* some direction. But he remained at a crossroads.

Up until yesterday, he and Django had been firmly focused on the gruesome murders of the three men: Anders Haugen, George Ross, and Chas Widdington. Those killings, even more than the murders of the women in Whitechapel, were unusual, even otherworldly. It made sense for the Society to be focused on those cases, given its interest in the occult. Besides, the Metropolitan Police, and now The City Police as well, were already employing a small army of personnel to investigate the women's deaths.

But yesterday, the idea that the men's and women's murders might be related had caused Scarlet to examine the photos of the female victims. And that had led him to the commercial area of London known as The Cut. There, a knife expert had informed him that the instrument responsible for the deaths of the four prostitutes might not have been a knife at all, but a pair of shears of ancient design.

The baffling question remained, however: *how* were the deaths of the women and the men related? The killings were wildly different in terms of modus operandi. For one thing, they were sex-specific—as murders of this type usually are—until you saw the dates and began to see a pattern, as Scarlet had done. But as far as he could tell, they were only roughly connected by those dates, in a way that could still be circumstantial. Yet his investigator's mind had picked up a thread and was now following it to determine if all seven killings—four female, three male—were linked.

Two other stubborn questions had presented themselves: (1) Were the different methods of deaths related to the sex of the victims, and if so, how? And (2) what in the world would an ancient tool have to do with four of the killings, and wild animals with the other three?

As it happened, Bilby's research would uncover the answer—or *an* answer—to only half of the last question. It would be some time before the other half of that question was answered, in a way that was nearly beyond belief.

It is the 2nd of November. Three men are sitting in the place they typically occupy to discuss a research request: the downstairs drawing room of Scarlet's house at One, Beaufort Circle in the Chelsea section of London.

Horace Bilby is seated in his favorite piece of furniture in the house—a circa-1770 English settee with its original rose-colored upholstery. Both of the other men are standing. At this moment, Scarlet can tell by the scowling look on Bilby's face that the little man is enjoying himself. Bilby is always in his element when the task at hand is, well, Herculean . . . and especially when the client is pessimistic about a favorable outcome.

"So you see," Pierce-Jones is saying now, "we were proceeding with one investigation, but suddenly the other has intruded itself. And we recently received information that opens up an entirely new direction in the second case."

"Yes, I see," Bilby allows. "When you say, 'the second case,' you mean the Whitechapel murders, which you hadn't initially been working on? Yes? And Mr. Scarlet, you say you've uncovered evidence which suggests that an obsolete tool might have been used on the four unfortunate women?"

Though Bilby continues to scowl as he says all this, Scarlet and Django can almost hear the unspoken final word: "Delightful!"

"I'd like you to start with the weapon," Scarlet tells Bilby now, handing him the sheet of paper with Hiram Joseph's drawing of the archaic shears. "I'd say the best place to begin is with museums and antique shops."

"We'll see," Horace Bilby answers cryptically, only glancing at the sheet of paper. "We'll see."

By which The Reader obviously means that he has his own ideas concerning how to begin his research.

CHAPTER 18

A Mother's Anguish

The next day, Saturday, the 3rd of November, brought Scarlet a much more mundane case to autopsy. Sad as it was, the death was apparently nothing more than a straightforward suicide. It was his on-call weekend, and he was summoned to the Yard at ten in the morning to perform the post-mortem.

The decedent's name was Evan Whincup, a twenty-one-year-old tosher or scavenger after valuables in the London sewers. These men worked with long rakes, aprons, and lanterns strapped to their chests, sifting through raw sewage and swarms of rats in the dark tunnels to find coins and booty they could clean up and take to the pawn shops. Going down in the sewers without permission had been outlawed by Parliament in 1840; but toshers had simply begun working late at night or early in the morning to escape detection.

Young Evan Whincup had hanged himself on Friday night, and his body was discovered the following morning, this morning, by his mother. Scarlet could certainly understand why a youth in such a trade would despair and end his life. But it was also ironic, as toshing was dangerous work which kept one on the edge of survival. Poison fumes frequently accumulated in the tunnels; and when the sluices were opened, a tide of noxious water and human waste could sweep away and drown a man. This young man had survived these everyday hazards, only to end his life through a rope and a rafter.

Whincup had done a good job. He had used a thick rope, so that the furrow in the skin of the neck was wider than it was deep. The ligature had caused blackening of the skin in a friction burn, a common occurrence. There was damage to fibers of the neck muscle and hemorrhage at the Sternal end of the Sternocleidomastoid muscle. The hyoid bone of the larynx was intact; and the ligature marks were slightly above the thyroid cartilage. This was an indication that the death did in fact occur by full suspension hanging and not horizontal (and homicidal) strangulation. Facial pallor was present, which was evidence that in this case, there was total arterial blockage.

Scarlet found nothing unusual in his post-mortem examination. It was obvious that this was a straightforward non-suspicious suicide by hanging.

He had finished sewing the body back up and was just placing a sheet on the corpse when he heard a shuffling sound behind him. He turned to see a thin woman standing a few steps in from the door, her hands neatly folded one over the other in front of her. He thought she was in her late thirties—or even her mid-thirties—though the tired and overworked look so common among London's labouring class made her look ten years older.

Despite her relative youth and unfamiliarity with this place, the stillness and dignity with which she held herself told Scarlet that this was Evan Whincup's mother. She looked completely out of place in the autopsy room, with her incongruous silk and linen dress's skirt (surely handed down to her from her mistress) and threadbare tweed coat. But her steady gaze informed him that she was totally unconcerned with the fact.

He was suddenly glad that she had showed up just this minute. The thought of her coming silently into the room while he was removing organs from her son's body was monstrous.

"I'm sorry, madam," he said. "You shouldn't be here."

"You've got nothing to be sorry of," said the woman, her facial expression tired but steadfast. Her voice was soft but just as steady as the rest of her demeanor. "I'm sorry that's my son over there."

This put Scarlet at a loss as to how to express his condolences. Obviously, he couldn't now say that he was sorry a second time. He settled for, "You have my sympathy . . . Mrs. Whincup?"

"Yes, that's my name. No 'usband to go along with it, though. Not these last six years." She nodded toward the shrouded figure. "Evan was my first, I was still sixteen when 'e came. I have three others, all girls."

"This must be difficult for you," Scarlet offered.

"Life's difficult, Doctor. Someone told me once that's the first sentence in the book the Buddhists read: 'Life is difficult.' We get by. Evan was always a sensitive and moral boy—things that people did bothered 'im, you see. And look where 'e is now, and only twenty-one years old."

"Mrs. Whincup, this isn't really a place you should be right now. Why don't you come upstairs to my office?" A thought struck Scarlet. "How did you find your way down here?"

"Oh, that was easy," said Evan Whincup's mother. "Everyone knows the authorities look into deaths when a crime's committed, or in suicides, like. I just 'eaded for the basement, where I thought you'd keep the bodies. Cooler."

When Scarlet took a step toward the door with his arm outstretched to indicate that they should leave the room, the woman said:

"No need to go upstairs. I'll be leaving. I just came to ask you something."

"I see. Would you at least like to sit down?" Scarlet asked, realizing too late that there were no chairs in the post-mortem lab.

"I know you found that my son 'anged himself," said Mrs. Whincup, ignoring the question. "But that isn't what killed 'im." She looked down at the floor.

"Something was bothering 'im. It was eating 'im up. I saw it and asked, but 'e would smile and tell me 'e was happy. But I know my boy, and I know 'ow 'e took things too 'eavy, like." She looked back up at Scarlet. "Took em to 'eart, you see."

"Did he have friends he confided to?"

"That's just it—'e did. Evan belonged to a group, an organization, with working-class boys and men, just like 'im. But it must 'ave done no good because . . . " and she merely gestured toward the shroud.

Then she looked at him.

"So what was it—? I don't even know your name."

"It's Scarlet. Dr. William Scarlet."

"What was it, Mr. Scarlet? What was it that killed my son? If you find out, will you let me know?"

She waited. When he didn't answer, she turned and walked with slow dignity out of the room.

Scarlet didn't move for some time. He was trying to decide whether it was deep grief or a distracted mind he had been talking to.

It was both, of course.

CHAPTER 19

A Blessed Sunday

n the 1888 liturgical calendar of the Church of England, November 4th was the Twenty-Third Sunday after Trinity. At St. Mary's Catholic Church in Chelsea, where Scarlet worshipped, it was the Twenty-Third Sunday in Ordinary Time.

All across London, worshippers in these denominations and others—indeed, those of all faiths and of no faith at all—breathed a sigh of relief this day. For this fourth of November could also be called the Fifth Sunday since The Whitechapel Murderer/ Jack the Ripper had last plied his trade.

At St. Mary's, William Scarlet was bowing his head in prayer for the souls of all the departed. His prayer included those whose murders he was investigating, and the young man whose autopsy he had performed the previous day.

At his house in Grosvenor Street in Mayfair, Django Pierce-Jones was contemplating the glass of vinegar in front of him with bleary eyes, trying to decide whether the supposed cure for hangover was legitimate. He decided it was all nonsense, and with a sigh of relief, poured the vinegar down the drain.

Horace Bilby was deep into a volume of *Rites and Rituals of Ancient Europe and Asia*, a smile on his face.

Sir Charles Warren, Commissioner of the Metropolitan Police

or Scotland Yard, was writing of his frustration to Sir James Fraser, his opposite number in the City of London Police. "We are inundated with suggestions and names of suspects," he wrote. Then he looked at what he had written and crumpled the piece of paper and threw it on the floor. He retrieved it a moment later, however, smoothed out the page with the edge of his hand, and began addressing an envelope to Sir James.

Scarlet's boss, Sir Edward Mallinson, Chief Surgeon of the Metropolitan Police, was reading the club's copy of today's *Times* over breakfast at the Reform Club, which had originally been made up of Radicals and Whigs but who were now men enrolled in the Liberal Party. Mallinson had inadvertently dripped egg yolk on the newspaper, and unable to wipe out the stain, was at the moment tearing off the blemished corner of the *Times* while no one was looking.

Mary Jane Kelly, the young Irish prostitute with the room at No. 13, Miller's Court was, despite the morning hour, already on her third pint of porter in a gin palace on White's Row in Spitalfields named The Full Measure.

The seven recent murder victims—four women, three men—slept on.

CHAPTER 20

In the Shadow of Fear

ive weeks had now gone by since the last murder of an East End prostitute. Instead of a return to normality, however, the districts of Whitechapel and Spitalfields seemed more than ever to be red in tooth and claw—as Tennyson had famously said about nature thirty-eight years ago.

Or if Lewis Carroll of fifteen years later was your cup of tea, things were getting curiouser and curiouser.

Sallow, furtive-looking men were seen lurking everywhere (where had they all come from?), as the entire East End apparently devolved into a bottomless pit of crime. And the public houses! Proprietors and patrons began fastening their gaze on suspicious types who ambled up to the bar alone . . . some with actual blood on their hands!

These men were followed when they left the premises, sometimes eluding their pursuers, but sometimes turning around to confront them. A few were even handed over to the police. However secret or dangerous these men seemed, however, they invariably turned out to be innocent of murder. Any blood on their hands was usually their own, or that of the animals they butchered in their trade.

Much worse in terms of man-hours wasted for both Scotland Yard and the newspapers was dealing with the deluge of letters that now poured in. It seemed like half the letters in England contained suggestions on how to apprehend the killer. The other half were apparently *from* the killer.

"Here's how to catch this stranger!" the first half screamed; while the second half mocked the reader with "I-am-Jack-the-Ripper-and-you'll-never-catch-me!" messages. And was there any red ink left in the stationery stores after these taunting notes had been penned?

Someone sent the Yard a human kidney. It was apparently from a woman who was a drinker, but nothing else about her could be determined. The police surgeons argued among themselves about whether the person who had removed the organ possessed any knowledge of surgery. Even the "drinker" part was disputed—current medical knowledge wasn't clear on whether kidneys were harmed by alcohol. (Dr. Scarlet thought they probably were, but didn't believe that the kidney thief was a doctor.)

Fear and paranoia now clouded the ability to reason, the same way fog obscured the alleyways and enclosed yards favored by the murderer.

On top of all this, people were still trying to tease additional information from the "Dear Boss" letter sent by 'Jack the Ripper' six weeks ago. *Boss* was an American term. Perhaps the killer wasn't one of ours at all!

Just the other night, a tall dark man was arrested in Whitechapel *while wearing an American hat*! His peculiar behavior had attracted the attention of fellow lodgers, and certain observations he made concerning the topic at hand aroused their suspicions. The Stones End police station on Blackman Street was alerted, and the Peelers brought him in for questioning. No word yet on what the man had said or what the officers decided about him.

In a letter to the Home Office, a person in Vienna, Austria was certain that the murderer was a "renegade socialist" trying to bring discredit on his former colleagues. But why would Socialists murder women like these, downtrodden members of society themselves and often thought of as outcasts? No one knew the answer to that question.

Social arguments like these spilled into the newspapers as well.

In the Godless brutality of the East London, said one letter-writer, conditions were self-perpetuating. Anyone growing up in such an environment was bound to be drawn to crime and vice. Why not re-channel some of the considerable funds being used to spread the Gospel and convert the heathens in Africa, and use the money closer to home?

But much had already been done, said another correspondent in answer to this letter—London had not been indifferent to the needs of the poor.

A third member of the public had a different opinion, and offered a longer-term view. The Whitechapel Horrors will not have been in vain if the public awakened at last to what conditions are like there. Otherwise, the borough was a place where it might almost be said that murders were bound to happen.

Through all of this, in spite of the more than month-long break from the killings—or precisely because the tension had continued to build—The Ripper was never far from people's thoughts. *When* he would strike again—not *whether*—was the question on everyone's lips. Crowds of people on the street corners, in the public houses, and in the parks asked it every day. And vigilantes acted on it every night.

Groups of concerned citizens had been active almost from the start of the Ripper murders, but others sprang up following the double murder of 30 September. The most prominent of these was the Mile End Vigilance Committee, formed by local Whitechapel tradesmen. As early as September 11 (three days after the murder of the second victim, Annie Chapman), they printed handbills and posters referencing the "Murders being committed in our midst," and offering a REWARD to anyone who gave information that ended by bringing the Murder or Murderers to justice.

Such vigilance committees were not the violence-prone vigilante posse seen in the American West, however. They were law-abiding, concerned with helping the police rather than meting out their own brand of rough justice at the end of a rope. Their stated aim was to "strengthen the hands of the police," and their patrols reported to the authorities anything suspicious they observed.

One aspect of the time *was* like the Wild West, however: the transformation of Whitechapel into a ghost town. At night, the people of the Borough disappeared from its streets—like departed souls who feared the darkness rather than welcomed it. Only locksmiths and patrolling policemen, it seemed, could be spotted out after dark on Whitechapel Road or Charlotte Street.

The prostitutes who hadn't left for safer boroughs had begun carrying knives. It was well known that only ghouls, or something worse, now stalked these streets. At least one housewife died, succumbing to fright in her home upon hearing of an unrelated murder.

Today, the 4th of November, was still Sunday, however—and while daylight lasted there was worshipping to be done. At St George's, for instance: the Church of England parish for the Borough of Bromley in southeast London. The church is only half a mile from the Chislehurst Caves, scene of an earlier worship ceremony seen in this story.

At the very moment St George's congregants were praying to the living Christian God, someone else was paying homage to an older (and much darker) personage.

This Friend of the Daughters of Night was not now with the rest of his group, however. He was alone. And he was at the Chislehurst Caves again not to pray, but to collect something left there for him.

Even though it was daylight outside, the caves were a perpetual realm of darkness, and he carried a lit candle as he approached the altar. Waiting for him on the stone table top was a pair of shears of an ancient design.

The believer picked the shears up, slid them into the deep pocket of his overcoat, and left the cave without further ceremony.

CHAPTER 21

The Clue to Difficult Problems

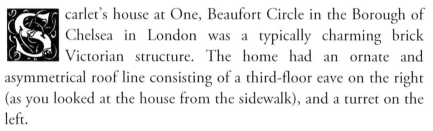carlet's house at One, Beaufort Circle in the Borough of Chelsea in London was a typically charming brick Victorian structure. The home had an ornate and asymmetrical roof line consisting of a third-floor eave on the right (as you looked at the house from the sidewalk), and a turret on the left.

This turret was small and octagonal, with a peaked roof and four windows. The fact that there were four rather than eight windows, which would have been customary in an octagon, meant that there was wall space between the windows. This interior space had been decorated with wallpaper.

To Scarlet's mind, the wallpaper was hideous. It consisted of a dark blue background, and cream-colored ovals which were under attack on all sides by a vast army of small pink flowers and intertwined yellow vines. The walls were otherwise unadorned by pictures or even gas lamps, for the light filtering through the windows this high up in the house was considerable. But it hardly mattered because no one ever went up into the turret. It was therefore the perfect place for committing the act of design sacrilege Scarlet had in mind.

His tools were on the floor beside him: a pail of whitewash which his man Jeffries had mixed, and a 5-inch paint brush. The desecration of just one wall would be sufficient for his purpose. He applied multiple coats of the whitewash (which is thinner than paint) to the wall, waiting between coats for it to dry. The entire process didn't take long.

Now, he stood in front of the finished project: a section of white wall which was the perfect blank slate for what he had in mind.

From a pocket he took out a carpenter's pencil. He was guessing the lead of the pencil was dark enough to show up on the whitewashed wall. It was.

He began by drawing a vertical line beginning as far above his head as he could reach, down to chest level. On the left side of this line he wrote, FEMALE VICTIMS, and on the right side, MALE VICTIMS. Something about seeing those words written out that way made him pause. He sensed a hint there of something significant. But his mind couldn't grasp what it might be, so he let it go.

He proceeded to write the particulars of the four East End prostitutes' murders—the so-called Ripper murders—on the left side of the vertical line. On the right side of the line, he did the same with the known facts concerning the deaths of the three men. He included the names, dates, locations, and times of the killings, and any relevant particulars concerning the wounds on each victim.

It was in this last item that the two sets of notes on the wall began to diverge. The women's murders included details about the mutilations of the corpses, while the men's killings listed not only the dismemberments, but evidence of the bite and tear marks present (importantly, these were different in each case). He left space at the bottom of the whitewashed area for any conclusions he might come to as to how the two sets of killings were related.

The idea behind this exercise was for Scarlet to be able to see the facts in front of him—larger than life-size, as it were. He hoped that a connection which he hadn't been able to recognize until now would step off the wall and into his brain.

But he wasn't going to simply stand in front of the wall waiting for a eureka moment to happen. At least, he wasn't going to stand there alone.

He placed the pencil on the floor and left the turret.

"So, your assumption is that the two killing sprees are connected," said Django Pierce-Jones. He was standing in front of the whitewashed wall with his left hand in his trousers pocket and his right hand hanging at his side, a Dannemann[*] held between his fingers. Scarlet, also smoking, nodded, The Roma King puffed on his cigar, adding to the foul atmosphere that now filled the small space.

Both of them stared at the wall for a few more puffs. Even in these conditions, visibility wasn't the problem. Making sense of what was written on the wall *was*.

How could such wildly different sets of killings be connected? Scarlet had two reasons for believing that they were. These were the types of reasons that any member of the city's police force could identify with: (1) the sudden violence being visited on the capital, and (2) the relationship of the dates of the women's killings and that of the men's.

London simply didn't normally experience this number of unsolved murders, especially in only two boroughs and the City. In the previous year, for instance, not a single murder had been committed in Whitechapel. Why were there suddenly *seven* of them recently committed there and in the two adjoining neighborhoods?

Scarlet was sure that the dates of the murders were significant. He had put that information up on the wall as well:

---

[*] A short, narrow cigar or "cigarillo," manufactured by Geraldo Dannemann's factory in São Félix, Brazil since 1873.

WOMEN'S MURDERS	MEN'S MURDERS
Mary Ann Nichols, 31 August	Anders Haugen, 3 September
Annie Chapman, 8 September	George Ross, 10 September
Elizabeth Stride, 30 September	
Catherine Eddowes, 30 September	
	Chas Widdington, 4 November

It was true that Widdington's death—the latest one—was an outlier, trailing by more than a month the double killings of Stride and Eddowes on September 30th. But Anders Haugen had died only three days after Mary Ann Nichols; and George Ross's remains were found just two days after the Annie Chapman killing.

Also, the Whitechapel Murderer/Jack the Ripper had also been inactive for five weeks now. To Scarlet, the hiatus in *both* sets of killings was also strongly suggestive of a pattern.

But he and Django still had no solid evidence of any link between the prostitutes' lives and those of the tradesmen. Where then was motive? Equally frustrating was the divergence between the "normal" murder method of throat-slashing (even with post-mortem mutilation), and the strange cases of men killed in savage animal attacks. And by creatures whose native habit wasn't the British Isles.

Could it just be a coincidence that these two killing sprees had occurred in London at the same time? The scientist side of Scarlet could accept that. But the supernaturalist could not.

"What are we missing?" he said.

Pierce-Jones answered immediately. "I don't think we're missing anything, really. It's the *outré* nature of the thing that has us stumped."

Scarlet's gaze might have been boring a hole in the whitewashed wall. But now he looked at Django.

"What did you say?"

"You mean that we're not really missing anything?"

"No, the other. You mentioned the *outré* nature of the thing."

"Oh, yes, I suppose I did."

"Could that be the answer? Or rather, part of it?"

"I don't get you, old fellow. The answer to what?"

"Maybe not the answer," Scarlet seemed to think out loud. "But the reason we're struggling to see the relationship between these two cases."

"If there is a relationship."

"Nonsense—I'm sure there is."

He thought for a moment. Then he said: "Of course! Stay here."

And he bounded through the turret door and down the stairs. He returned in a moment with a slim, one-shilling book in his hand. Django could read the title. It was *Tales of Mystery, Imagination & Humour; And Poems,* by Edgar Allan Poe.

"I believe it's in "Murders in the Rue Morgue," said Scarlet, placing the book on a table and flipping quickly through the pages. He stopped and began skimming the text on one page.

"Yes, here it is," he said, and kept his finger on the page as he looked back at Pierce-Jones. "This is the great amateur detective, C. Auguste Dupin, speaking to his friend, the narrator of the story. You remember, it's all about the strange recent murders of a wealthy old woman and her daughter in Paris."

And he began to read aloud the following:

It appears to me that this mystery is considered insoluble, for the very reason which should cause it to be regarded as easy of solution—I mean for the outré character of its features. The police are confounded by the seeming absence of motive, not for the murder itself, but for the atrocity of the murder. They are puzzled, too, by the seeming impossibility of reconciling . . . the facts. They have fallen into the gross but common error of confounding the unusual with the abstruse.

"Do you see it?" he asked. But his gaze went back to the book before Django could answer. He continued reading the passage:

But it is by these deviations from the plane of the ordinary, that reason feels its way, if at all, in its search for the true. In investigations such as we are now pursuing, it should not be so much asked 'what has occurred,' as 'what has occurred that has never occurred before.' In fact, the facility with which I shall arrive, or have arrived, at the solution of this mystery, is in the direct ratio of its apparent insolubility in the eyes of the police.

He looked up at his friend.

"We've been puzzled in precisely the same way as in the story," he said. "We too have been 'confounding the unusual with the abstruse,' as Poe says, by the bizarre manner of the men's deaths. We haven't been able to see a way to connect that unusual fact with the more prosaic killings of the East End prostitutes—if I may call it that—however horrible they've been."

"Yes, I grant that," replied Pierce-Jones.

"But that's our best clue that they *are* related."

"Now you've lost me."

"Don't you see? It's the outrageous nature of the men's killings *in connection with the women's*, that should have alerted us all along. The dates show it clearly. Think about it. If people suddenly started dying at the hands of wild animals in London, out of nowhere as it were, we would think it odd, but we'd find some ordinary explanation behind it fairly quickly. We said it ourselves earlier: we would trace it back to animals recently escaped from a zoo, or a shipment of creatures from abroad. In either case, Bilby would have discovered the fact easily. But that isn't the case here at all. We have no explanation whatever for it, ordinary or otherwise."

"Again, granted."

"Well, that shouldn't be possible," insisted Scarlet. "Unnatural killings like these don't just start up from the blue."

He might have said supernatural killings if he'd thought of it.

"There has to be a reason for them—and the fact that they started occurring in tandem with unusual killings of women in the East End is a hint as to that reason. Poe in his story has given us a rule that we can follow in this case: that the level of difficulty or bizarre nature of the occurrences makes the solution not harder but easier."

He considered what he'd just said, and gave a half-laugh. "We might even call it, generally speaking, 'the clue to solving difficult problems.' Do you see now how it works out in these two sets of cases?"

"No," said Django, with a somewhat sad look of bewilderment. "I'm afraid I don't."

Scarlet considered, then said:

"I'll put it this way. One set of extraordinary murders would, understandably, stymie us. But *two* sets are leading us in the right direction."

"How so?"

"They are telling us that the men's deaths are in response to the women's murders." He paused. "Of course, why the killings of Haugen, Ross, and Widdington occurred in that strange way is something we still don't know."

"Or even the fact," added Pierce-Jones, "that three men might have had something to do with the murdered women. I mean, instead of a single killer as everyone has been assuming up to now."

"Exactly," agreed Scarlet. "And we still don't have an answer to the two biggest questions of all. First, why were these men in particular targeted?"

"And the second?"

"That one's even stranger," answered Scarlet: "Is someone standing up for these women after death, and if so, why?"

Now, for the first time since the killings began—and despite these unanswered questions—Scarlet felt a new and undeniable sense of hope.

CHAPTER 22

The Men in Question

he belief that the two sets of killings were related—that the men's deaths, in fact, were in response to the prostitutes' murders—provided a sense of direction that the Scotland Yard physician-detective had been lacking. He knew from experience that once a centrally important clue had been gained, the true nature of a crime and its motives usually emerged clearly and at once, like a ship suddenly sailing into view out of a fog bank.

They didn't have that clue yet. But he knew how to proceed, and that was just as important.

He could now apply a standard law enforcement tool of a death investigation: digging into the victim's history. Every investigative policeman knew the method: learn about the victim's associations and movements just prior to death, and you'll be one step closer to solving the case.

It was time to find out more about Anders Haugen, George Ross, and Chas Widdington: who they were and how they lived their lives. If there was a link between their deaths and the murdered East End prostitutes—as Scarlet now believed there was—that is how he would discover it.

Ingunn Haugen was a tall woman of around forty-five with a square face, a thick neck that tapered not at all, and dirty-blonde hair in braids. Her hands were large and strong-looking, her eyes of steely blue. If someone had said to the average Englishman or Englishwoman, "Imagine a working-class Norwegian housewife," Ingunn Haugen might have been the result.

When she answered Scarlet's knock on the door of her rowhouse in Peckham Road, she didn't look surprised. The same was true when he identified himself. The woman only nodded and stepped aside to let him in.

Scarlet immediately had two thoughts in quick succession. First, that her English might be limited. And second, that the two months since her husband's death might not have dissipated the shock and numbness of it all.

The interior of the house gave the impression of a woman who attended to her duties whatever life threw at her. The tiny front room was spare and neat and looked meticulously clean. He didn't hear the sound of children in the rooms up the stairs, nor was there any evidence of them anywhere. The atmosphere of the small rowhouse told a story of self-reliance, resolve, and the acceptance of responsibility. Mrs. Haugen herself looked unmovable.

She had indicated to Scarlet the only piece of furniture in the room with any fabric on it: a small chair with a tufted back and matching cushion. His hostess chose an uncomfortable-looking straight-backed chair painted in a garish green that looked like it would improve anyone's posture in seconds.

"Vould you like something to trink?" she asked the instant they sat down.

Scarlet demurred. Instead, he immediately expressed his sympathies.

"Yes, tank you?" said Mrs. Haugen, with the pronounced upward inflection so characteristic of the Norwegian language. Her expression didn't change. The pause that followed indicated that she was waiting for him to tell her why he was here.

"Mrs. Haugen, I understand that your husband was employed as a loader and unloader of wagons at Baldroy's Transportation Company. That's near here, isn't it?"

"Ja," she nodded, then pointed. "Up on the Peckham Road a vays. Mr. Haugen could walk dere from here."

"Did he spend much time with friends from work?"

"Nei, he did not. Vell, to go out for a trink sometimes at the pub. Dat's all."

"How did he spend his leisure time? I mean, his time away from work."

"Here, at home. And valks. He liked to go for valks in the evening after vork."

"Did he have any close friends, Mrs. Haugen?"

"Nei. Just the people from church."

"You both went to church regularly?"

"Oh, ja. Ve go every Sunday. Ve are good Lutherans."

"He was religious, then?"

Ingunn Haugen looked steadily at Scarlet as she replied. "Mr. Haugen vas a moral man. He didn't like sinners."

"I see," said Scarlet. "And these walks you mentioned. Forgive me, but were they often to Green Dale Fields, where his . . . where he was found?"

That, as last, seemed to have touched a nerve. The woman took a deep breath and only nodded, not looking at Scarlet.

"How often did he take these walks, Mrs. Haugen?"

"Alvays, he take dem. In nice weather or even in the rayen, he still valk."

"Do you happen to know if he ever met anyone on these walks?"

"Nei, I don't know. Who? Who would he meet in the park?"

"So your husband didn't associate with anyone?"

"Ah, dat's what you're asking. He belonged to a group of vorking-class men, like him. A club. Dey get together now and then, not regular."

"Well, I asked earlier if he had any close friends, and you said—"

"Not close friends, I don't think. Just a . . . " she searched for the word "*social* club, like the vorking-class men have. Dat's all."

"What's the name of this social club?"

She merely shrugged.

Scarlet considered what else he might ask Ingunn Haugen. Aside from her obvious reserve in the face of his questions, it was clear she didn't know much about her late husband's life outside of the home. If Anders Haugen had associated with a criminal element, she probably wouldn't be aware of it. Given how his activities were probably pretty well accounted for between his nearby place of work, his walks in the evening, and occasionally visiting his social club, there was probably little time for that kind of thing anyway. Could his "walks in the park" be an excuse for something that might have gotten him in trouble? Scarlet doubted it.

There didn't seem to be much left for Scarlet to do, except to thank the woman for her time. So he did so, adding:

"Mrs. Haugen, is there anything I can do for you?"

Her briefest of head shakes, followed immediately by her standing up from the chair, was all the answer that was needed.

To Scarlet, the air outside the house seemed wonderfully fresh and sustaining.

"I never drink spirits in a public house," Nell Ross announced.

She and Scarlet were standing on the sidewalk in front of 40 Alie Street in Whitechapel, where the Ross family lived. The two had met by chance: Scarlet on his way from Ingunn Haugen's home in Camberwell, and Mrs. Ross coming from the local pub, The Hart and Hare.

"All right, then," said Mrs. Ross when Scarlet explained the reason for his visit, then turned and walked up the steps to the building's front entrance. She stumbled over the threshold— "Stubbed me toe," she explained over her shoulder—then led the way up the stairs, where the family had rooms on the second floor.

Scarlet had had no reason to doubt her statement regarding spirits. The woman was, however, soaked in beer. She was carrying a two-quart galvanized pail or "growler" filled with that beverage home from the pub. Once in the hallway, he could smell beer evaporating through the pores of her skin.

She unlocked the door to her home and walked slowly across the floor to place the growler on the nearest table. Then she turned and faced him, her hands on her hips.

"Well?"

Her eyes were sad and suspicious in equal measure. 'Bereft' was the word that came to Scarlet's mind.

George Ross's widow was short and round, and her face was very red at the moment. She'd had considerable trouble mounting the hallway stairs. In between labored breaths, she had informed Scarlet (again, over her shoulder) that her daughter Emily was at her flower-making job, and her two boys were at her sister's house with their cousins.

He thought the remarks were by way of excusing the fact that she was drunk in the middle of the afternoon—that she didn't need to be caring for her children at the moment. She swayed slightly in front of him, waiting for any reply.

"May we sit down?" Scarlet asked when it became obvious that she wasn't going to be the one to mention it.

She nodded solemnly, then said: "Like some tea?"

"No, thank you, Mrs. Ross."

When they were seated, he began.

"I'd like, if I may, to ask you some questions about your husband. First, I want to say that I'm sorry, ma'am, for what happened."

At the mention of her husband, Nell Ross's face changed. The sadness seemed to slip away, and the suspicion became anger.

"My husband was forty-six, Mr. Scarlet. D'jew know that?"

"Yes, I did, Mrs. Ross. I'm terribly—"

"He worked hard, George did."

"I can see that. He was obviously a good provider."

In reply, his hostess waved her arm widely, indicating the room where they were sitting. The Ross home consisted of three rooms. The largest was this room—what the family would call the "parlour." It contained the following: two soft chairs, a dinner table with five seats arranged around, a sewing table on the other side of the room away from the door, a fireplace with an arm for a kettle or a pot, and two beds on wire frames that were placed underneath the single window.

A doorway with fabric on curtain rods in lieu of a door led to a kitchen; and the same arrangement sufficed for the entrance to what was probably the bedroom. Scarlet surmised that the boys slept on the beds by the window here in the parlour, and that the bedroom held beds for Mrs. and Mrs. Ross and the daughter.

There were a few bare spots in this room where he guessed that pictures or tables with lamps—perhaps a spinning wheel—had once stood before they were pawned. The home was certainly modest enough, but it showed that the family could afford to rent and maintain rooms. The death of Mr. Ross as breadwinner two months ago, however, would have begun to change all that.

"Mr. Ross was a street vendor, wasn't he?"

Nell Ross nodded. "A costermonger, with his own cart," she said proudly. "Oysters 'n eels, and a bit a' fish. Twenty years and more, my George worked his territory. Leman Street 'n Cable Street 'n St George's Street—all them streets 'tween here and the docks. The High Street down at the river too, sometimes. This area ain't much, Mr. Scarlet, but it's a good place for that trade, right where they bring in the fish. My George knew that, even as a young man."

"Your husband was successful in his business, then?"

"Oh, aye! He always provided for me and the kiddies, did George."

"His work must have brought him into contact with a number of people at the fish market and the docks."

"'course, it did, all them years."

"Was he on upstanding terms with everyone? Any financial problems?"

Mrs. Ross leaned forward in her chair.

"My George was a good man, Mr. Scarlet," she said. The challenge in her voice was clear. "A moral man."

"I'm sure he was, ma'am. I'm sorry if it sounded as if I was implying anything. What I meant was, did he have any enemies? Anyone he didn't get along with down at the docks?"

"No," answered Mrs. Ross, looking at the floor and shaking her head as she thought. "If he did," she added illogically, "it wasn't his doin'." She leaned further forward and stared intently at Scarlet, as if struggling to keep him in focus. "George was no troublemaker."

She was slurring her words more, and her mood seemed to be darkening.

"What I meant was, the docks are well known for being a dangerous place. Do you know if he spent any time there at night, Mrs. Ross?"

The question seemed to surprise her. "I do," she said. "And the answer is, he didn't. Always home after work, 'cept to stop in the pub sometimes. Brought his money home, too . . . right here," she said, pointing to the floor.

"Was he ever threatened that you know of, anything like that?"

She laughed. "Where do you think you are, Mr. Scarlet? This is Whitechapel. What d'you think it's like here? You come down here, askin' questions. This's a jungle . . . a jungle! You fight for everything, you do, every minute. And your kiddies don't have no childhood, either.

"Was my George threatened? Of course, he was, and robbed too! And every man that can't stand up for himself would be swallowed up, like that!" she told him angrily, unsuccessfully trying to snap her fingers.

"Did anything ever come of these—?"

Now she was pointing at Scarlet in the chair opposite her.

"Beasts!" she said. "Savages! This slum is nothin' but a jungle, and they crawl out at night. Aye, and in the daytime as well. They come out to do their hunting. And not only men—the women, slatternly and debauched, 'orrible to look upon. Fuckin' the gents in their fancy frockcoats in the alleys. Everyone, preyin' on honest people." She began to cry. "Oh, George, my George!"

Scarlet stood and took a step toward her chair.

"Don't you!" she cried, putting her hand up, palm out. "They killed my husband, you!" she wailed. "They took him—a mob of 'em—and tore him apart. For nothin'! Why? Why? My poor George!"

"Mrs. Ross," Scarlet began, hardly knowing how to broach the truth, to remind the woman of the nature of her husband's death. "There is evidence of an animal attack, it's almost certain—"

"Piss off!" she said, waving both arms this time. "Animals? They're human wolves—those are the animals that killed my husband." She mumbled something else he couldn't hear, then trailed off into silence, staring unseeing into one corner of the room.

After the interviews with the two widows, the fact that the third man, Chas Widdington, had been a bachelor seemed a blessing. In the late afternoon, Scarlet visited the United Service Club in Pall Mall, where Widdington worked as a waiter and in the club's library.

But he gained little information. Apparently, Widdington was a loner who didn't socialize with the other members of the service staff.

Back in his office, Scarlet looked over the notes of the Widdington case, which were spread out on his desktop. Widdington had purchased a Great Eastern Railway ticket for the 04.23 train leaving on the morning of his death for Witham, Essex. That was obviously why he was at Liverpool Street Station so early that morning. Scarlet got up and walked over to the map of England on his wall.

Why Witham? It was a town in the low country of Essex near the North Sea, well off the beaten path. Witham wasn't a place you'd stop off to see on your way to somewhere else, like visiting

Canterbury on your way to the beaches at Margate or before you shipped out with the fishing fleet at Ramsgate.

But was that, in fact, the whole point? Did Widdington deliberately choose that part of Essex because it would be difficult to find him there? Was he running from something . . . and if so, what? And if that was the case, why hadn't Anders Haugen and George Ross also tried to get out of London?

He consulted the dates of the three men's deaths again. Haugen was killed two days after the Nichols woman's murder; and it was exactly the same with George Ross, who died two days after Annie Chapman was killed. Then, following the double murders of Elizabeth Stride and Catherine Eddowes in the early hours of September 30th, there had been a five-week break before Widdington's death—which was also the exact amount of time the Whitechapel Murderer/Jack the Ripper had paused (ended?) his killing spree.

Was Widdington's gruesome death—so similar to the two other men's—in response to the double murder in September, whatever the reason for the delay? Could it be that Haugen and Ross simply didn't have time to get out of London before they were killed, as Widdington was obviously planning to do?

What was the link that tied all these deaths together?

And then, a chilling thought: Had the Whitechapel killer not yet chosen his next female victim, after which yet another man's life would be taken as well?

As Scarlet sat at his desk pondering these questions, a realization slowly coalesced in his mind, the way snowflakes in a swirling storm might momentarily combine to create what looks like a human figure. But this was not his imagination working, but his memory.

He wrote a short note, then sent for an office messenger.

It was dinner time when he arrived at Django Pierce-Jones's house at 14 Upper Grosvenor Street in Mayfair, a half-block from the northeast corner of Hyde Park. You could see a section of the park from the parlour's windows. In fact, that was where Django was standing when Scarlet entered the room.

"Got your note," said Django, crossing the room to shake Scarlet's hand. "Dinner will be ready in a moment. Hope you haven't eaten."

"Actually, I'm ravenous," Scarlet replied, realizing that he couldn't remember when he'd last eaten.

"Good. You mentioned in your note that you've been taking time out from your new painting career to interview the men's widows."

Scarlet laughed. Django was obviously referring to yesterday's whitewashed wall in the turret, where the two of them had considered the clues in the two cases.

"Yes, I spoke to Haugen and Ross's widows," he said. "And I visited the club where Widdington worked."

"I imagine speaking to the two women must have been difficult for all concerned."

Scarlet agreed with that thought, though now he shook his head.

"I can't imagine what they're going through," he said. "The Norwegian woman is like ice . . . and no, I'm not making a joke. It's her way, I imagine. Putting up a strong front, you know. Ross's wife seems wounded. She's been blindsided, poor woman, and has taken to drink. The home looks like some of the furniture has been pawned as well. It's a sad business all round."

"Did you learn anything?"

"Well, that's the interesting part," replied Scarlet. "Despite the difference in the way they're coping with their husbands' deaths and the way they spoke to me they both said the same thing. Used the same word, in fact. I only realized it afterwards, when I was thinking back to the conversations."

"What was it?"

"They both said, 'My husband was a moral man.'"

"I see," said Django. "Coincidence?"

"If twice is a coincidence, what does that make three times?"

"What do you mean?"

"Three days ago, I performed an autopsy on a young man named Evan Whincup who committed suicide. His mother came to the Yard just as I finished the post-mortem. She said to me, 'Evan was a sensitive and *moral boy*'—that things people did upset him."

Django considered this information. "Interesting," he said.

"Mrs. Whincup told me that something was bothering Evan. 'Eating him up,' was the way she put it. But she said he had denied it and told her he was fine."

"So, there's somehow a question here of morality?"

"I don't know," Scarlet answered. "But it seems odd that it was mentioned in regard to three out of these four men—if we can now include Evan Whincup in our list. And I think we should."

"Why is that?"

"Because of something else both Anders Haugen's widow and Evan Whincup's mother told me. I didn't pay any attention at the time, but it might also be a common thread. They said both men belonged to a club—a 'working-men's organization,' is how they both put it. But neither of them knew the name of it."

"What about George Ross's wife? Did she mention it?" asked Django.

"No. But she was drunk, and too angry for me to be able to question her sufficiently. She said it was the people of Whitechapel who tore her husband apart. She called them human wolves."

"Do you believe that?"

"No, of course not. . . . And as for Widdington, there was no one at the United Service Club where he worked who could tell me whether he belonged to any social organization. He lived by himself and was apparently a loner."

"Or maybe he was lonely," countered Django, "and joined a club for that very reason."

"Perhaps."

"So, what do we have?" said the Roma King. "An organization of working-class men that neither of the women you talked to—the wife of one man and the mother of the other—knew much about. And, given the apparently upstanding nature of these men, a group that might concern itself with some moral issue?"

"Like temperance or a missionary society? Hardly the kind of organization that would get mixed up with murdered prostitutes, wouldn't you say?"

Django had no answer for that.

Scarlet hoped it wasn't too late when he reached Maud Whincup's dwelling in White's Row, Spitalfields after dinner at Pierce-Jones's house. He could have come earlier; but if he hadn't accepted Django's dinner invitation, he'd have gone the entire day without eating.

East London—slums like Whitechapel, Spitalfields, and Bethnal Green—was the part of the city some people called "darkest London." Maud Whincup's house was one of the reasons why people said it. The house was located in a tiny square with a dozen dwellings opening onto it. The square sloped downwards on both sides toward the middle, where a narrow trough served as a dumping stream to carry away dirty laundry water, and perhaps worse.

The entrance to Mrs. Whincup's home was a dark opening with the appearance of a cave or barn stall, though it did have a door. Scarlet noticed that there was only one window on the first floor, and none at all on the second.

He knocked on the door and it was opened immediately, telling him that Evan Whincup's mother had probably been watching him approach from the window. She wore a large shawl draped over her head and shoulders, which nevertheless probably wasn't much proof against the November night. He could see that the small fireplace on the opposite wall of the room was unlit, and in fact there were no coals in the grate.

The woman facing him was indeed the same one who had confronted him in the autopsy room at the Yard three days earlier. But the violence of her sudden grief on the day she had found her son hanged was gone, though the rawness of the emotion hadn't left her eyes.

She still carried as well the look of a lifetime of weariness that added years to an otherwise comely woman in her mid-thirties. The years of motherhood and household service that must have started when she was fifteen or sixteen had drained Maud Whincup of all color. Scarlet could see that she must have been fair to begin with; but any blush in her face and warmth in her hair had leached away.

She was thin and of middle height; and she held herself with the same dignity she had exhibited in the morgue three days ago. Her eyes were the only part of her that had resisted the stripping away of youth and color and expectation. They were large and blue, and though still filled with grief, they look out at Scarlet with a knowing and intelligent expression. She clearly recognized him, though her eyebrows were still raised as they had been when she opened the door.

"Mr. Scarlet. Good evening."

"Good evening, madam. Please excuse an unannounced visit. I wonder if I might speak to you?"

"About my son?"

"Yes, about Evan. It's rather indirectly related to an investigation."

"I see."

She didn't move, however. Scarlet wondered if she was making up her mind.

"I'd very much appreciate any help you might be able to give me."

Mrs. Whincup closed her eyes for the briefest of moments. "Of course," she said, and stepped aside.

The room, the only one on this floor, was small and cramped with bare walls. It did double duty as a kitchen and sitting room, with all the necessary furniture, counters, utensils, and other paraphernalia. Paths led through the profusion of items to a stairway. Upstairs—probably again in a single room—there would be beds for Mrs. Whincup and her three daughters. Wet clothing hung on a clothesline that ran the width of this room.

"Laundry day?"

"Every day, with four children, Mr. Scarlet."

Four children. She had included Evan, then.

They were still standing just inside the front door. Though Mrs. Whincup hadn't asked him to sit down, and hadn't inquired whether he'd like tea—courtesies in any class of English society that were so common as to be nearly unconscious—Scarlet felt more welcome here than in either of the homes he'd visited earlier today. As difficult as her son's suicide must be for her, it seemed that Maud Whincup wasn't going to inflict her pain on him. She seemed patient and respectful. He could think of many of the "better" class that could have benefitted from those virtues.

"I won't be long, Mrs. Whincup. When you visited me the other day, you said that something was bothering Evan. 'Eating him up,' is how you put it. You don't know what that was?"

"I do not. When a young man is that age, he no longer confides in his mother about certain things. I'm sure you understand that."

"Yes, of course. And you said, I believe, that he had friends, though apparently they couldn't help with what was bothering him. Is that accurate?"

"It is."

"You mentioned that Evan and these friends were part of an organization of some kind. Was it by any chance a working men's group or club?"

"Yes, Mr. Scarlet, it is. I'm afraid I don't know much about their activities, however. It's a group that concerns itself with bettering the lots of unfortunate women.

"Really," she added, shaking her head, "there are so many of these organizations, you have to wonder whether they're getting in each other's way."

"Do you know the name of the club?"

"Yes. It's an odd name, really: They call themselves the Friends of the Daughters of Night. I suppose that's because of the work they do rehabilitating women of the streets, the Daughters of the Night. At least, that's the only sense I can make of the name."

It was indeed a blasted odd name, thought Scarlet, though he didn't say anything about it.

"One more question, if I may, Mrs. Whincup. Do you know if Evan saw or learned of anything recently that might have upset him? Something involving the organization's work?"

"D'you mean having to do with the Ripper murders?"

"That, or anything else."

"I'm sorry, doctor. I don't."

"And do you happen to know where I can find the group? Is there an address you know of?"

"I'm afraid I don't know that either." Her eyes were slightly sad. "I'm sorry I can't be of much help to you, Mr. Scarlet."

"On the contrary, Mrs. Whincup. You've been very helpful."

As Scarlet bid the woman goodbye and left the tiny square, he was sure that was true.

Even if he didn't know how just yet.

CHAPTER 23

Nothing New Under the Sun

Scarlet had less than a day to wait, however, before Horace Bilby—The Reader—provided a startling answer.

Again this morning, just as five days ago, Scarlet, Pierce-Jones, and Bilby were meeting in the downstairs drawing room of Scarlet's house. Bilby had sent a telegram the evening before to the house, telling Scarlet that his research was complete and that he was ready to report his findings. The news didn't surprise the Scotland Yard surgeon. He well knew the speed and thoroughness with which the indomitable Bilby could gain the information he'd been tasked to find.

It soon became apparent, however, that the little man would be delivering any news he had through bouts of sneezing. The weather had been cool and damp—a typical London November—and if Scarlet remembered correctly, Bilby was allergic to mold spores, a fact which always made him miserable in the fall.

Otherwise, he and Django were prepared for a standard Bilby performance, which usually involved sharing the most startling information with perfect blandness. They had decided long ago that it was a testament to The Reader's level of ability. Like all great artists, an essential part of the performance was making it all seem effortless.

Bilby had two books open before him on the oval coffee table in front of the settee. These were the oversized account ledgers in which he recorded his voluminous notes, always in a crabbed hand that scribbled anywhere and everywhere, obliterating the faint lines on the pages and any margins. The fingers of his right hand, in fact, were always so ink-stained that they might have been tattooed.

"As you know," he began, and sneezed three times in quick succession.

"Excuse me! This blasted season." Stuffing his damp-looking handkerchief back into his pocket, and resentful of his own interruption, he continued:

"It was ingenious of you, Mr. Scarlet, to suggest starting with the weapon which you believed may have been used on the victims in the Whitechapel Murders. The same murders," he added, "which you suspect might have some connection with the men's deaths which you and Mr. Pierce-Jones have been investigating. It really was the most effective way to start my research."

Scarlet nodded slowly as he refilled Bilby's teacup. It was best not to make any comments at this stage. If you asked how in the world he'd found this or that tidbit, for instance, The Reader's pride in his research would invariably lead to a long and winding road paved over thickly with his ingenious methods.

"We're speaking, of course," Bilby continued, "of the primitive design of the shears shown to you by the cutler. As you recall, this design was unusual when compared to the modern variety of shears. In the older instrument, the entire tool was cast from a single piece of iron, razor-sharp along the blades but curled back on itself in a loop to form the handle. The extraordinary sharpness of the blades, in fact, was another characteristic of this ancient design."

Another sneeze.

"In *these* shears, however, as opposed to modern ones, both the inner and outer edges of the blade can cut along their length. They could therefore be used to either puncture or snip as today's shears or scissors do, but also to cut along either the inner or outer edge. One could even begin slicing by using the shearing action, then close the blades and continue to move downward, turning the cut into something like blunt force." Bilby demonstrated this action with an invisible set of shears he was supposedly holding.

"I believe that the dual nature of the cut was, in fact, a characteristic of one of the wounds of a female victim you looked at, Dr. Scarlet? An ingenious design, really. We lose so much with our modern innovations, don't we? None of us would even know about the unique qualities of this marvelous instrument without the drawing you were given. And, of course, a bit of concentrated research.

"Now," the little man continued, "I believe you already have some idea of the provenance and historical periods in which this tool was used. It was invented in Egypt around 1,500 B.C., and used over the centuries until the Romans invented hinged shears during the reign of Nerva or Trajan. Further research on this particular design, however, narrows things down considerably in terms of the period of common use. In this case, that was almost certainly in Greece, during what we call the Golden Age."

"Around 500 B.C. or so?" asked Django.

"More or less," allowed Bilby. "Let's be a bit more specific, and say sometime between 490 and 404 B.C. That is, from the defeat of the Persians at Marathon in the Persian War until Athens herself was defeated by Sparta in the Peloponnesian War. That's a convenient time frame for us."

"But why would anyone today want to remake an ancient agricultural tool used in Golden Age Greece?" asked Scarlet.

"Well, obviously in this case, for murder," Bilby replied blandly. "Whatever the motive, the connection with this weapon to ancient Greece is almost certainly determinative."

He shook his head, clearly not satisfied with the statement he had just made.

"It's stronger than that, actually. You see, I believe that is the very reason for this tool. It was that conjecture, in fact, which led me in the right direction. That is why your instinct to begin with the weapon was such a stroke of insight, Dr. Scarlet. These shears were made to be used ritually you see."

Pierce-Jones sat up straight at the statement. Scarlet asked quickly:

"What kind of ritual?

Bilby looked at his notes briefly, then up again at his listeners.

"One of the cults common in Golden Age Greece," he began, "were worshippers of the Moirai—what we call the Fates. You know about the Fates?" When both men nodded, he continued. "As you know, Clotho was The Spinner, who spun the thread upon which every human being's life depended. Lachesis measured the length of each thread, that is, the life span of every person. The third Fate, Atropos The Unturning, cut each thread at the length that was indicated, causing that person's death. Three goddesses who controlled everyone's life on Earth.

"The particular cult connected to these shears worshipped Atropos, the cutter of the thread, who never yielded, by the way, in her task of ending anyone's life at the appointed time. Hence 'The Unturning.' This cult was particularly concerned with morality in ancient Greek society. They had local groups—chapters, we might call them—in all the major cities: Athens, Sparta, Corinth, Megara, Thebes—even Smyrna in Asia Minor, which today is in Turkey. They worshipped Atropos while calling upon her to rid society of wrongdoers of any kind: thieves, the immoral, those who took graft or beat their slaves, even unfaithful wives."

"But not unfaithful husbands?" asked Pierce-Jones.

"Apparently not," answered Bilby, missing the irony.

Scarlet: "What about prostitutes?"

"Oh, yes," Bilby replied. "Very definitely prostitutes. This cult prayed to Atropos to carry out her duty, as it were. To strike down the undesirables who were polluting the society. To cut their thread of life."

"But if the length of their lives had already been measured," Pierce-Jones put in, "how could these cult members—with the goddess's help—strike the wrongdoers down because of any immoral behavior?"

"Evidently, that was a point of logic which eluded this cult. According to their beliefs, Atropos would appear in answer to their call. She would affirm their 'duty'—and even provide them with the weapon to carry out their necessary executions."

"Atropos's shears," Scarlet finished the thought: "To cut the thread of these people's lives."

Bilby nodded enthusiastically.

"Precisely! Given the Whitechapel murders of street prostitutes, it's possible—perhaps probable—that a modern group has resurrected these ideas and is using this ancient weapon to rid London society of evildoers. In this instance, the notorious East End ladies of the night. Perhaps they've resurrected the worship of the goddess as well."

"How in the world can you make those assertions?"

"From the shears you yourself showed me, Mr. Scarlet," answered Bilby, "and the fact that they are being used exclusively on prostitutes. That, and the name of the organization."

At the blank looks that he received, The Reader elaborated.

"The information you sent me last night, Doctor, after you'd spoken to the woman whose son committed suicide. She told you the name of the group, and that her son was agonizing over something he was involved in recently or that he'd seen. Well, it all fell into place, you see."

"How so?" said Scarlet.

"She told you the group's interest is in rehabilitating London's women of the streets. But I think their purpose is very different.

"You see," Bilby concluded, 'the organization's name is the same one as the worshippers of Atropos in ancient Greece—The Friends of the Daughters of Night. It's the same vigilante group."

CHAPTER 24

Dull Onto Death

Thursday, the 8th of November 1888 was a cold, dull day, with rain that night. Throughout the day, Mary Jane Kelly worked equally hard at staying warm and remaining drunk. She was more successful at the latter, which, she knew well from experience, made the former easier.

At least (she reminded herself) she had some flesh on her, which helped. As she had once told a friend in the same profession: "I ain't one of them Kitties with nothin' on 'em, so a man has no ass to grab hold of." Yes, she was a putain. But she was also twenty-two and big and attractive in a way men liked. She knew she was a nice bit of laced mutton—hefty and solid and hot, so that men sometimes liked to bury their face between her thighs while asking her to close her legs.

"Well, it's called 'leg-business,' ain't it?" she asked out loud now to no one, and laughed at her cleverness.

Lying on her bed, she studied the ceiling and thought of how nice it was to have your own jook to take a gentleman back to, and not have to do yer business outside with the rest of the cattle. Her single room at No. 13, Miller's Court in Spitalfields wasn't much, God knows. But it was warm enough when you had some coals in the grate, and dry, which was no small thing on days like this. And *private*—that was the thing.

Like any whore, she appreciated having someone like Joe Barnett as her man to bring in money for expenses and such. But Joe was out of work right now, so there was nothing coming in from that direction.

He'd been angry recently when she let a fellow Kate stay in the room for a few nights and had packed himself off to a lodging house. Well, *fuck him*! Though she missed talking to him (when he wasn't angry or she wasn't too far in her cups), she had to admit that him not being around made things easier for her to conduct business in the little room.

She liked Joe well enough; but a man was a man, and she could always find one of those. Which of them wouldn't like a tall, blonde, robust young girl like her with her lilting Irish accent and big, firm titties? Not every man wanted to live with a woman who was on the game, that was true. Well, if they didn't, fuck them too!

She laughed again. She *did* fuck 'em, whether they shared her room or not. And they paid for the privilege!

She didn't like this Ripper business, though. *That* gave her the wobbles.

Funny thing, though. She made Joe read the newspaper stories to her about the murders; and if he didn't bring home a paper, she would get one herself. From time to time, when heavy drinking brought on the wobbles, she would ask him, out of the blue like, if they'd caught the murderer. Then she would half-listen to his angry, jealous tirades sayin' he didn't want her out on the streets. But she'd have another gin, and her temptation to agree with him and change her behavior would slide away. Besides, what was she supposed to live on without him bringing in any money?

By dusk, she was ready to get back on the knock. Joe was out of the way at his lodging, or more likely, looking for work. If he was shaving down his shoe leather, she knew that would take him all of the day and some of the evening, too. And someone had to pay the rent, which was again in arrears.

Dorset Street was busy and a little too out in the open; but any of the streets off Brick Lane were always good bets for doin' the business. On a gloomy day like this, an alleyway entrance with the darkness behind it was almost as good as nighttime for advertising your intentions.

The alley itself would serve, if she decided her gentleman wasn't gentleman enough for her to bring him back to her place. If she took a right on Wentworth Street, and another right on Thrawl Street, there was an alley that was in a sweet spot between Whitechapel High Street and Dorset Street, both of which featured good foot traffic.

She wasn't one to fish for the beaus (too young), nor the drunks (she wasn't a roller). It was always a gentleman Mary Jane was looking out for, especially one with a watch chain in view. That was a guarantee that he'd be able to afford her rate of 8d.—quite reasonable, she thought, for a young piece like her. She'd rather trade tail quickly to get enough to drink than raise her price and stand outside in the buggerin' cold, negotiating.

All she could find this evening, however, was a clergyman looking for a Tuppenny Upright in the alley behind her. Only a barrack hack would actually charge 2d., of course, and she insisted on her eight pence, even for a stand-up. The earwig was at least tall enough, so she didn't have to crouch down while up against the wall, which was dreadful tiring on the legs, especially if the fellow was slow in finishing. Tuppenny Uprights weren't no favorite of any of the wagtails, anyway, because you was always dry, and there's only so much spit you and your wencher can come up with.

This one was quick—thank God for small favors—and she had her 8 pence, enough for some wine at the Rose and Crown. She didn't linger there, though. She had an idea that Joe might stop by her room in Miller's Court, so she hurried along the few blocks between the pub and her place in the early darkness, getting back there by 6.00 p.m.

She was right, because Joe showed up just after 7.00. When she answered the knock and saw him in the doorway, she wished that she'd been able to afford more wine. She'd have liked to have been in a softer mood and glad to see him.

As it was, she realized he was more like an acquaintance to her now. She studied his narrow face, boyish haircut, and thin moustache, and realized that there wasn't enough of a man there to interest her, just someone to bring money into the household . . . if you could call her place in Miller's Court that.

But it turned out to be all right. Joe wasn't angry anymore, and she found herself thinking of the encounter as a friendly visit. He had no money to give her, of course. But it was all civil and proper like. He asked how she was keeping on, and she inquired about his success (there was none) in his job prospects. He only stayed fifteen minutes or so, and they said their goodbyes with something like affection.

As soon as Joe had left, however, and without any event to explain it, a mood of darkness and gloom began to descend on her. If she'd had any drink in the room, she'd have taken some now to head off the bad feelings, but there wasn't none.

Sometimes it happened this way. She saw her life with sudden clarity. She'd had a decent enough upbringing in Limerick. But now, at the age of just twenty-two, she was living in one of the worst streets in London—with her rent of 4 shillings now six weeks in arrears—and working as nothing but a common street whore.

She was suddenly sick at heart at the life she was leading, drunk part of each day, a habit which she knew changed her into someone she didn't like and didn't want to be. She knew this feeling always ended in one of two ways: with her dreaming about getting enough money to go back to Ireland, or thinking about bloody suicide.

Was it knowing that it was finally over with Joe that was making her feel this way? Or was it the Ripper, who cast his shadow over the entire East End and especially women like her? Among her other thoughts was that she'd have to buy the papers herself now that Joe was gone, to read about whatever killings came next.

All these bad thoughts drove her out of the house. She decided to visit Elizabeth Prater, the woman who lived above her. Prater's husband had left her five years ago, and she now worked in a doss house as a charwoman. She was also known for not practicing no judgments against the street walkers who made up a large percentage of Miller's Court.

The visit turned out to be a good idea, because Elizabeth cheered her up with a reminder that tomorrow, Friday the 9th, was the Lord Mayor's Show. This was the day when the new mayor drove in state to the Royal Courts of Justice in the Strand to be administered the oath of office.

"I want to go to the Lord Mayor's Show!" Mary Jane declared loudly.

"We shall go together!" Elizabeth agreed, and the two women laughed heartily, even without the help of any drink.

That situation was soon remedied, however, at least on Mary Jane's side.

Her conversation at Elizabeth Prater's house was brief, and she was on the street again by nine o'clock. By 10.00 p.m., after another stand-up in an alley, she had enough money to visit the Horn of Plenty, which is where she was drinking with friends and having a meal of fish and potatoes when Daniel Barnett, Joe's brother, showed up. He asked if he could speak to Mary Jane apart from the others, and she agreed.

But it was the other Mary Jane—the one who came out when she was drunk—who followed him until they were sufficiently far away from the table.

"I won't!" her friends heard her say loudly, and again: "I won't! I'm through, and you can jus' go back and tell him."

Daniel made a pleading gesture and tried speaking.

"No!" Mary Jane shouted, then broke off the conversation.

She returned to the table and her friends.

As Daniel walked toward the door of the public house, Mary Jane shouted after him.

"Tell your brother I'm through with immoral courses!" she told him, and laughed.

CHAPTER 25

A Maddening Time . . . and a Plan

". . . the organization's name is the same one as the worshippers of Atropos in ancient Greece," Bilby had just told Scarlet and Pierce-Jones. "It's the same vigilante group."

Scarlet knew at once that it had to be true. For whatever dark or misguided reason, this secret society —The Friends of the Daughters of Night—had reconstituted itself here in London. The original version had dedicated itself to ridding Greek society of those they considered immoral. In that task they had worshipped one of the Fates, Atropos, calling upon her to help them in their work.

Atropos the Unyielding—the cutter of the thread of life.

Today's Friends was apparently a group of working men who had taken the same task upon themselves, this time to rid London of its notorious prostitutes. And incredibly, like the older group they were using the ancient shears of Atropos herself to carry out their task.

The men who had been savagely killed recently—Anders Haugen, George Ross, and Chas Widdington—had all belonged to the club, as had the young suicide, Evan Whincup. Scarlet was certain of that fact with regard to Haugen, Ross, and Whincup, and it was a reasonable enough deduction concerning Widdington.

The two investigations, as he had suspected, had indeed converged. He and Pierce-Jones knew now how and why the four

East End prostitutes had been murdered, and who had actually done it. Not a Jack the Ripper, but a series of "Jacks": one after another, carrying out their secret organization's warped pledge to cleanse society of what they considered an evil that had to be stopped.

But to Scarlet, this knowledge was as maddening as it was revealing. For he and Django had no way of knowing when the Friends of the Daughters of Night would strike again, nor who their next target would be. And they were still completely in the dark about who or what had brought about the terrible deaths of Haugen, Ross, and Widdington: the members of the Friends who had carried out the prostitutes' murders.

For the conclusion was inescapable: some other individual or group was enacting a series of savage revenge attacks against these men who were themselves guilty of murder. And Scarlet and Django hadn't a clue yet as to who that was.

They now had two seemingly impossible tasks. First, to prevent another prostitute's murder. And if that failed, to stop the horrible revenge killing of the murderer which would inevitably follow.

And they had no idea of the time frame in which they had to accomplish one or the other of these tasks.

Scarlet knew that they had to move as quickly as possible. As soon as Bilby was finished with his report, he outlined their next moves.

He told Bilby that he wanted him to look more deeply into the lives of the dead men. If there was any evidence that would reveal the meeting location of The Friends of the Daughters of Night, they needed to find it.

At the same time, The Reader was to dig for any contacts that Haugen, Ross, or Widdington had made at or outside of work—especially with any person or group who may have subsequently followed or stalked them. The last of the three dead men, Chas Widdington, had been trying to leave London via the Great Eastern Railway the morning he was killed at Liverpool Street Station. They could assume, then, that among the three Friends who had carried out murders of prostitutes, he at least had been stalked.

Given Widdington's failed attempt to leave London, it seemed likely that the plan was for each of the men to disappear after they'd committed their murder: Haugen of Mary Ann Nichols, Ross of Annie Chapman, and Widdington of Elizabeth Stride and Catherine Eddowes. If that was the case, then their deaths resulted from one of two possibilities: either they couldn't get away in time, or the person or persons responsible for killing them was too powerful for their escape plan ever to have worked. Of the two, the latter seemed the better bet, since it wasn't likely that all three of the men had bungled their plan to disappear.

For Scarlet, there was also a more worrisome thought: Was it the police whom the men were trying to escape from, or a more primitive form of justice? For if the vigilante group was tied to an ancient goddess whose task was to end human lives, why couldn't— or *wouldn't*—there be someone or something else involved in avenging those same women's deaths? And whatever that entity might be, was it beyond Scarlet and Pierce-Jones's ability to understand or fight it?

At any rate, their immediate task was clear: to prevent the murder of another prostitute.

That task might be an impossible one, however. The Friends of the Daughters of Night seemed to follow no discernible schedule for their ritual killings. And Scarlet and Django had no way of infiltrating their ranks so that they could be present at their next meeting. Their one consolation was that the "Ripper" murders had stopped completely—the last one had been at the end of September, nearly six weeks ago.

Also, by now the streets of the East End were patrolled constantly by three separate groups: The Metropolitan Police, the City of London police, and the vigilance committees that had sprung up. How could Scarlet and Django accomplish what dedicated police professionals and people who knew their own neighborhoods intimately couldn't?

But six weeks is an impossible amount of time to function at a fever pitch; and as was inevitable, the vigilance of citizens and even of the police was diminishing. New eyes, on the other hand, often meant new discoveries. It was an idea that had been in Scarlet's mind recently, and now it was time to put it into practice.

He kept a set of maps of London in his home, in addition to the official set in his office. Now, he took out a section of Cram's 1887 London map from his map filing cabinet and placed it on the dining room table. It was a detail of sections 88 and 89 of the larger Cram map. At this resolution it was wonderfully detailed, showing every street, road, square, park, and railway line—and of course, the serpentine curve of the Thames—from Acton in the west to just beyond London Docks in the east. That latter area, at the right-hand edge of the map, showed precisely the neighborhoods in Whitechapel and Spitalfields that he was interested in.

"Look here," he said to Django. "This is where all of the women's murders took place," and he drew an inverted triangle on the map with the same carpenter's pencil he'd used to write on the whitewash three days ago. The center of the triangle was the intersection of Whitechapel Road and Commercial Road—the two central arteries of Whitechapel commerce. From there Whitechapel Road continued westward, first as Whitechapel High Street, then Aldgate, which shortly thereafter met Bishopsgate Street, which ran north and south. This intersection of Aldgate and Bishopsgate was the southernmost and lefthand point of the inverted triangle. The second point, farther east on the map, was Buck's Row, where Mary Ann Nichols had been killed. The third point—its northernmost tip—was where Bishopsgate met Commercial Street.

In the crowded streets and lanes of the map showing portions of Whitechapel, Spitalfields, and a corner of The City of London, the triangle revealed a sharply delineated area. Seen this way, it was a striking demonstration of how compact the "Ripper's" killing zone was. From Mitre Square (Catherine Eddowes) to Buck's Row (Mary Ann Nichols)—the murder sites farthest away from each other—the distance was only nine-tenths of a mile.

"My God," said Pierce-Jones as he looked down at the map.

"I'd say this is the area where we can expect the next murder attempt," offered Scarlet.

"I agree. But what about timing? How do we know when one of the Friends will strike again?"

"We don't," Scarlet admitted. "But I think we can devise our strategy in terms of heading off the next murder based on this triangle. The Yard has all the major streets and roads within this area well covered—saturated with men, in fact. They're also out in force in secondary streets like Hanbury, here, Wentworth, here, and Middlesex, here, and of course, near all of the alleys and courtyards that are favorite spots for the women to take their customers."

Still peering closely at the map, he asked Pierce-Jones: "What would you say are the worst areas in this part of London? No, let me rephrase that: what are the neighborhoods that have large populations of prostitutes, and also offer the most opportunities for concealment *inside* a premises where business can be conducted yet not seen?"

"I'd say Buck's Row because of the row houses there," Django responded, "and Miller's Court off Dorset Street, which has rooms, tenement houses, and shops, with entrances to all of them from the courtyard."

Scarlet placed two fingers at those points on the map: his right index finger on Buck's Row, his left on Miller's Court.

"And if you had to concentrate on only one of those two to focus on, which one would it be?"

"Miller's Court."

"I agree. But why do you say so?"

Pierce-Jones answered immediately.

"Buck's Row was the site of the first killing, that of Mary Ann Nichols back in August. We have to assume that the Friends won't repeat the site of a murder—they haven't done it up to now."

"Yes, that's my thinking exactly. Miller's Court it is, then."

"For what?"

"Let's go," was Scarlet's only answer.

It was 3.38 p.m. on November 8th.

CHAPTER 26

A Jook Of One's Own

By 11.09 that night, Mary Jane Kelly had had enough wine. It was beginning to make her quarrelsome, which made her decide she'd had enough conversation as well. She stood up from the table, said goodbye airily to her friends with a wave, and stumbled out the front door of the Horn of Plenty.

The public house was at the corner of Dorset and Crispin Streets in Spitalfields, which was perfect for her. Her room in Miller's Court was a mere two-minute walk away.

In fact, Crispin Street was a good place to conduct business. It was a busy thoroughfare, but narrowed at a sharp angle where it intersected with Bell Lane. If she stood at the corner of Crispin and Bell, clients would practically be herded into her lap, she thought with amusement.

She knew from past experience that the best place to stand was at the corner of White's Row where it joined Bell. There, she would be noticed by anyone walking down Crispin Street; but if the law showed up, she could turn around and walk away down White's Row and they might never even see her. And she'd be just around the block from Dorset Street and her room in Miller's Court.

Mary Jane had just turned the corner from Dorset onto Crispin Street to put her plan into action, when she saw an acquaintance, George Hutchinson. She crossed the street to talk to him.

"'Evening, George," she said; and in an attempt to get on his good side, added: "I ain't seen you around. Will you lend me sixpence, love?"

"I can't," Hutchinson replied. "I have spent all my money going down to Romford."*

"Good morning," said Mary Jane (which of course was inconsistent with her original greeting, though it was approaching midnight). "I must go and find some money."

She left Hutchinson standing under the gas lamp outside the Queen's Head Public House and continued down Crispin Street. No sense in dawdlin' talking to a friend, she said to herself, thinking again of the three weeks the rent was in arrears.

Her strategy paid off almost immediately. As she leaned against the bricks of a tenement house at the corner of White's Row and Bell Lane—a pose which is as good as wearing a sign advertising her intentions—someone tapped her on the shoulder. She turned around. And, lor', if this wasn't a bloke who fit the bill exactly!

She could see right away that this one weren't no gentleman. But he was dressed respectable, which told her something. He was shorter than her at five-feet-six or so, but solid-looking, like he worked in a physical trade. Mid-thirties, she'd say. His clothes weren't fancy but they were presentable enough: he wore a dark green suit, a light-colored waistcoat, and dark felt hat with the brim turned down low in the middle. His face was on the dark side, which probably explained why he wore his hat that way. He had on workman's boots rather than shoes. Top-wise, he sported a clean white linen collar and black tie . Yes, respectable enough.

She noticed that he had some kind of parcel in his left hand with a strap around it. And then she saw it: a gold watch chain leading to a small waistcoat pocket on his right side. Mary Jane was unconcerned whether he uses the watch at work, or was wearing it tonight to look more like a gentleman—it was clear evidence that he had enough money to pay for his preferences.

---

* A town in East London in the borough of Havering.

He leaned in to tell her confidentially what those were, and they both burst out laughing. His accent was thick and sounded Slavic. He didn't phrase his requirements as a question, as most of 'em do, in the way of asking if she was amenable. For him, she thought, it was simply the fastest and easiest way to come to an understanding, and no jabbering about in the street where anybody could see ya. She supplied the next line, which was also part of the age-old script they were making use of.

"You ain't from the pussy posse, are ye?"

She expected him to laugh, but he didn't. In fact, he didn't say anything. She noticed that his eyes were hard-looking, and thought he might be impatient. 'No more talkin,' like, 'let's get down to the business at hand.' She wanted to be sure she understood what that business would be, though.

"And it's full personal you want?" she asked. That meant sexual intercourse rather than masturbation. Another standard question from the script.

"I said zo, didn't I?" And now his voice had a hard edge as well.

Well, she couldn't blame 'im. The gent knew what he wanted, and had told her. He had no more interest in chit-chatting here on the corner than she had a moment ago with George Hutchinson. This was commerce, pure and simple.

She told him her price and where they would do the business. There was some pride in the way she said it, on account of she had a jook of her own and they wouldn't have to use an alley. He just nodded slightly. Gawd, no muckin' about, this one, she thought.

Then he said something surprising.

"Why don't I get growler that we take back to your place? You like beer?"

She smiled. This time there was no need for her to reply.

They began walking up Crispin Street towards the Queen's Head. Her friends back at the Horn of Plenty three blocks away wouldn't be surprised to see her if she showed up there with a monger, of course. Still, it was better this way.

As they were walking, Mary Jane shivered.

The shawl she was wearing wasn't much protection against the high-30s night temperatures of early November. Anyway, shivering from time to time is part of the game when you're out on the streets, idn't it?

CHAPTER 27

A Brief Recess in the Court

carlet called out to the driver of the cab to let them off at the corner of Commercial Street and Dorset Street, a half-block from Miller's Court. He and Pierce-Jones then walked down Dorset Street past the entrance to the court, getting the lay of the land. Dorset Street consisted of only one long block between Commercial and Crispin Streets, so it didn't take long.

It was around half-four in the afternoon now of another dull, cold day, and the dismal faces of the buildings on the block just added to the gloom.

At this time of 4.30 p.m. on the 8th of November, Mary Jane Kelly was lying on her bed in her room at No. 13, Miller's Court. She was looking up at her ceiling, at first musing about her relationship with Joe Barnett, then thinking about her considerable attributes for attracting other men. Then the wobbles had come when she thought once more of Jack the Ripper. Her Tuppenny Upright later that afternoon in the alley; Joe's visit in the early evening; her chat later with Elizabeth Prater; and her leaving her room a second time after 11.00 p.m. to visit her friends at the Horn of Plenty before going back on the streets, were all in the future.

Unlike Mary Jane's lack of concern about the hour, Scarlet and Pierce-Jones felt that time was pressing on their mission, though they didn't know whether that pressure was gentle or urgent. There was only so much reconnoitering they could do in Miller's Court and environs, and only so many questions they could ask here.

If nothing happened after a day or two of this undercover work and they got no leads, they wouldn't be able to remain in the neighborhood. They were conspicuous in dress and social class, certainly—though it must be admitted that men like them came to this area knowing exactly what they would find here, so they weren't that unusual a sight. Asking questions about the Ripper murders, however, was another story entirely. Equally bad would be scaring off the killer before he had a chance to do anything incriminating.

And how were they to tell the difference between a gentleman with whoring on his mind, and a member of the Friends of the Daughters of Night here to carry out his society-cleaning errand? The question and the situation were both damnable. It was a bad business all round.

But this place had seemed their best bet as to where one of the Friends killers would show up next, and now they had to make the most of it. After walking along the sidewalk on both sides of Dorset Street, they strolled casually through the small arched doorway and into Miller's Court. They did this consciously, trying to look for all the world like two Mayfair gentlemen slumming. There was also the fact that the more furtive they looked (given their supposed reason for being here), the less anyone peering out their window and down at the courtyard would consider them out of place.

If anything, the long, barren courtyard was more dismal in appearance than Dorset Street itself. There was a chandler's shop* at No. 27, Dorset, the building next to the courtyard's entrance. At that spot, a dark passageway about a dozen feet long led into Miller's Court.

The courtyard proper contained a small separately standing room on the right, a water pump on the far-right wall, and tenement houses on both sides with doors and windows facing the central

---

* Candle-maker.

open space. The only illumination at night would be the single gas lamp on a post just to the left as you emerged from the passage into the yard. It would provide plenty of light to see the doorway to the small room near the entrance; but the rest of the courtyard must be shrouded in gloomy darkness at night.

Scarlet was acutely disappointed by what he saw. They certainly couldn't remain here, strangers in an open courtyard where surely everyone knew everyone else. There was little doubt that prostitution was a necessity in this neighborhood, and that Miller's Court must be a near-perfect venue for it. The courtyard provided protection from prying eyes that was almost as good as an alley. Better yet, the houses here—and the single room at No. 13—offered private spaces, again without the chance for anyone on the street to see a doxy and her client entering them.

Given their exposure standing in the wide-open yard, the two of them would have to observe any activity from beyond the arched passageway on Dorset Street. From there, there would be no way for them to see what went on once a gentleman had entered the passageway and then disappeared into the courtyard with his companion. Unless there was a scream, they wouldn't know whether that same gentleman emerging from the square a short time later was a quietly satisfied customer, or someone who had just committed murder.

If they knew someone who lived in Miller's Court, on the other hand, they would be able to get information from *inside* the courtyard. It was a solution beyond them at the moment, but it bore thinking about.

They decided that they could at least double their surveillance by splitting up. The single entrance to the courtyard (via the passageway) opened up onto Dorset Street. From there, anyone turning left would reach busy Commercial Street at the next intersection, while heading in the opposite direction would bring them to Crispin Street. Now, Scarlet headed to the larger thoroughfare of Commercial Street, while Pierce-Jones undertook surveillance on the smaller street.

By standing on the corners, they would both be able to see all of Dorset Street. They could follow a suspect whichever direction he took as he left Miller's Court—or apprehend him if they saw him running away. They would switch locations every hour. It was a Thursday night, thank goodness, so both streets were busy enough that they weren't worried about being noticed.

The thought occurred to both of them—though they didn't mention it to each other—that their presence in this neighborhood may be nothing but a misguided goose chase. After all, the killer had two entire boroughs to choose from, if the activity of the Friends up to now was the clue they thought it was. There was also the City, for he might decide to return there. And suppose he didn't plan to strike tonight at all?

Yet Scarlet couldn't shake the feeling that something was imminent. In his mind, Evan Whincup's suicide was a vital clue. It was true that the Friends of the Daughters of Night hadn't struck for five weeks. Yet something was bothering Evan greatly.

If all was quiet within the secret organization, why had he been so disturbed? Not for the first time, the thought occurred to Scarlet that the young man may have been the designated killer this time and had agonized over what he had to do, taking what he considered the only way out.

By nine o'clock, however, Scarlet knew he had to devise a different plan. They simply needed eyes inside Miller's Court: someone who lived in the courtyard, or at least in the neighborhood and had a reason to be there. He decided that one of the street urchins who populated the area whatever the hour would be the perfect choice.

There was a steak and chops house, Dolly's, two-and-a-half blocks away on Tenter Ground off White's Row. Anyone who lived in this neighborhood would know it. Scarlet and Pierce-Jones could get off the street by dining in the restaurant, with whomever they might find to reconnoiter Dorset Street and Miller's Court reporting to them there.

They soon found their spy. He was sitting on the sidewalk outside McCarthy's Chandlery at No. 27, Dorset Street, the building next to the passageway. With his back propped up by the brick wall, he was eating an apple and watching the steady flow of people passing on the sidewalk and in the streets. He looked to be about eleven.

The lad was dressed in a coarsely-woven wool shirt of natural color, black full-length stockings, brown shoes, and black knickers with sewn-on braces. His black coat had the collar turned up, but remained unbuttoned. His outfit was topped by a round felt cap, with blonde hair underneath that had been not trimmed but shaven, probably, thought Scarlet, because that was more economical. When the two men stopped before him, he looked up suspiciously.

"Good evening," Scarlet said, smiling.

"'evenin', sir."

"My name is William Scarlet, and this is my friend, Django Pierce-Jones."

"You a gypsy?" the boy asked the latter immediately.

"I am, actually. Half of my heritage, at least. Why did you ask?"

The boy nodded. "Yeah, you only half look it. Your name sounds gypsy-like, though."

"And may we ask your name?" said Scarlet.

"Georgie Foster."

"You're out a bit late, aren't you, Georgie?"

"I'm thir'een," said the boy, and left it at that.

Scarlet crouched down to be on his level.

"And what do your parents think about you being out on the street?"

"I dunno. I don't think they're 'ome."

"I see. Do you know this area, Georgie?"

"Rather! I live in there," and the boy gestured with his thumb toward Miller's Court.

Scarlet and Pierce-Jones looked at each other, eyebrows raised.

"Well, Georgie Foster," said Scarlet, "would you like to earn a shilling?"

"Fer what?" The look of suspicion intensified.

"My friend and I are interested in the comings and goings of gentlemen entering the houses in Miller's Court."

Georgie considered that reply, then took a deliberate bite of his apple and chewed it slowly.

"You coppers?"

"Actually, yes. I'm a doctor employed by Scotland Yard."

The boy digested this information along with his recent bite of the apple. "You mean you're interested in the wagtails and their gents?"

"Well, yes—that's exactly who we mean."

"That's all right then," announced Georgie Foster, and the suspicious look disappeared. But apparently, he wanted to make double-cross-yer-heart sure that he and his benefactors understood each other. "I can keep 'em all straight," he warned. "Not to the minute, see—I ain't got no watch—but I can let ye know the comins' and goings. That what yer lookin' for?"

"It is," replied Scarlet. "And Georgie, this is important. If you hear or see anything that worries you, I want you to let us know right away."

"You mean if I hear a scream, like?"

"Well, let's say anything unusual. Or if you see something out of the ordinary."

"Where will you be, then?"

"Do you know Dolly's Restaurant, a few blocks over on Tenter Ground?"

Georgie nodded.

"That's where we'll be. It's just after nine now. Can you keep a lookout for a couple of hours and then come to report to us there? At eleven sharp? You'll have to ask someone the time, of course."

"Nah. I'll hear the bells of Christ's Church, won't I?"

Indeed, Scarlet realized, he would.

The three of them shook hands. Solemn, like.

At approximately one minute past eleven o'clock, Georgie Foster showed up at Dolly's. He gave his employers a run-down of the comings and goings of Miller's Court during the last two hours. According to their spy and lookout, three of the rooms in the tenement houses opening up onto the courtyard were used by prostitutes to bring home customers.

"Also the room at No. 13, that sits on its own just inside the passageway," Georgie added. "That's Mary Jane's room. But I didn't see nobody goin' in or out tonight."

The rest of the activity in the courtyard—carnal and otherwise—sounded routine and mundane, with nothing that they could recognize as being out of the ordinary. Scarlet paid Georgie his shilling and bought him a meal. They sat with the boy as he wolfed his food down, with a few looks around as though he thought it would disappear if he didn't.

It was nearly midnight when they left the restaurant.

Mary Jane Kelly and her client, having bought their growler of beer at the Queen's Head, made their way through the passageway to No. 13, Miller's Court at 11.40 p.m.

Scarlet and Pierce-Jones missed them by fifteen minutes.

CHAPTER 28

A Cry in the Night

As Scarlet and Pierce-Jones retraced their steps along Dorset Street, they could see the steeple of Christ's Church directly in front of them and on the other side of Commercial Street. The clock in the church's spire read 12.02. And so Thursday, November 8th became Friday, November 9th, with nothing but the silent church tower to herald the new day. Here in Spitalfields, that day was as poor and cold and wet as the one that had just ended.

They had the choice of spending the rest of the early morning continuing their dull surveillance, or going home. Georgie, despite his view of himself as a denizen of the night, was struggling to keep his eyes open after his substantial meal at Dolly's. And of course, it wouldn't do to keep the boy from getting home where he belonged.

Scarlet also had his duties at the Yard to attend to this Friday. With a plan to check in later that morning by messenger if anything came up, he and Django took separate cabs to their homes.

THREE INVITATIONS TO MURDER

Inside her room at No. 13, Miller's Court, Mary Jane Kelly was singing. She often sang when drunk, and now she was very drunk indeed. She'd had a considerable amount of wine earlier at the Horn of Plenty. And she and her new benefactor had started on the growler of beer before they even neared the courtyard; and now the container was considerably emptier than it had been when it departed the Queen's Head.

Mary Ann Cox, a prostitute who lived in the last house at the far end of Miller's Court, but who wasn't in the habit of bringing men back to her room, heard the singing. At about 11.45 p.m., she had seen Mary Jane entering her room with what Mrs. Cox knew was a customer.

To her practiced eyes, he was of the common breed of tail-chaser: short, with a sooty complexion and dressed shabby-respectable like, in a dark overcoat and black felt hat. Perhaps his complexion was why he turned his head away when Mary Ann and the pair passed each other, his hat pulled down to hide his face.

"Good night, Mary Jane," Mrs. Cox had called out.

Kelly, very drunk, had been barely able to reply, but she said 'good night' in return. As Mrs. Cox continued through the courtyard to her building (she wanted to warm up a bit before going back out on the streets), she heard the young Irishwoman's lilting song:

"Only a violet I plucked from my Mother's grave . . ."

Jane Buttery, another resident of Miller's Court, heard it too. She was actually staying with a friend tonight on nearby Thrawl Street. Before retiring for the night at the friend's house, however, she realized she hadn't brought a letter her nephew, now serving in the Navy, had sent her recently.

Her hostess was a close friend of the young man and Jane

wanted to read the letter to her. The friend's house was only three-tenths of a mile from Jane's room, so she had returned to Miller's Court just before midnight to fetch the letter. She heard Mary Jane Kelly singing as she entered the courtyard.

Once in her room, however, Jane had fallen asleep in her rocking chair while taking a moment to rest, and so it was after 1.00 a.m. that she awoke and started back to her friend's house.

It was raining hard by then, however, and she decided it was silly to venture out in such a downpour. Standing in the tenement building's doorway waiting for the rain to let up, she noticed that the lights were out in Mary Jane's room at No. 13. She knew this because it was difficult to see how hard it was raining with no lights behind the water slanting down. She went back upstairs to her room and sat in the rocking chair to read the letter a second time as she waited for the rain to stop, and once again fell asleep.

Mary Jane Kelly's friend Elizabeth Prater, who'd she visited early the previous evening, was having the opposite problem. An insomniac, she couldn't sleep, despite having drunk a considerable amount of wine in the hope that she'd be able to do so. Finally, at around 3.30 a.m., she began to doze lightly.

The letter from Jane Buttery's nephew fell to the floor with a soft sound as Jane opened her eyes and sat up. Her cat was sitting by the rocker, looking up at her. Had the cat woken her up? Then she heard it again—the sound that had awakened her: a woman's scream, and a female voice crying "Murder!"

She hurried to the window. The gas lamp near the entrance of the courtyard was out, so Jane thought it must be after four, the hour when the lamp was usually turned off. She listened again to what had seemed a faint yet close-by cry of that awful word. But there was no other sound. She petted the cat and went to her bedroom, and was soon asleep again.

In her own "two-pair back" place directly above Mary Jane Kelly's room, Elizabeth Prater was suddenly awake from her dozing. She thought she had heard someone—a woman—scream "Murder!" She had the feeling she hadn't been asleep long, so it was probably sometime around four a.m. She was sure she hadn't been dreaming. She listened, but heard nothing more.

The scream didn't disturb Elizabeth greatly. You heard that kind of thing frequently coming from the tenements that looked down into the courtyard, or from Dorset Street.

It probably didn't mean a thing, she told herself, and went back to sleep.

John McCarthy, owner of the chandler's shop at No. 27, Dorset Street and the landlord of No. 13, Miller's Court, had decided a few days ago to give Mary Jane Kelly until the end of the week. That was today, Friday. It was time to tell his lodger that he needed something of the three weeks' rent that was in arrears. He wasn't a hard man. Surely, anyone could judge that by the fact that he'd allowed the arrears to accumulate for that amount of time, couldn't they? But 29 shillings was nothing to laugh at.

McCarthy wanted to deal with the issue early because today, November 9th, was the Lord Mayor's Day, and he planned to observe the procession as it made its way from the City to Westminster. The boundary of the City of London at Middlesex Street was just half a mile from here; and Westminster, where the ceremony would end, was only four miles away. He intended to make his way to Aldgate and start walking the route, looking for a good perch from which to watch the parade.

He also considered it beneath a landlord to confront a tenant and ask for the rent himself. So he sent his assistant, Thomas Bowyer, a pensioned soldier and jack-of-all-trades around McCarthy's properties. The forty-one-year-old Mr. Bowyer knocked on Mary Jane Kelly's door at 10.00 a.m. There was no answer.

Unwilling to return to his boss without results, Bowyer decided to peek in the window. Whores' hours weren't the commonplace kind, he knew, and it was possible that Mary Jane had gone to sleep in the early hours of the morning and was sleeping it off. Two of the four panes in the window next to the door were broken—the bottom and top ones on the right side—so he was able to stick his hand in the bottom window and draw back the curtain slightly.

Mary Jane, whom he knew and recognized, was on the bed, all right. But he was confused by what he saw.

She seemed to be wearing a white dress or nightgown, but he couldn't tell where that garment ended and what he thought was a red blanket began. That had a crazy-quilt pattern, with small patches of white mixed up with larger areas of red. There were also chunks of something red—he didn't know how else to describe it—on the table beside the bed.

It was only when he noticed that Mary Jane's face was mostly red too that Bowyer understood what he was looking at. It wasn't a red blanket. The woman had been thoroughly butchered. Her entire abdomen was carved open, and some of the organs had been removed and placed on the bedside table.

He ran back to McCarthy's shop.

"I knocked at the door, but got no answer," he told his employer. "I knocked again and again, and received no reply."

"Well, all right, then," said John McCarthy, and began to turn away, satisfied for now that Mary Jane wasn't home to give him any of the rent money.

But Thomas Bowyer grabbed him by the arm.

"I passed around the corner by the gutter, about where there is a broken window," he continued, determined to tell the rest of his story. "I put my hand through the broken pane and saw two pieces of flesh lying on the table. The second time I looked, I saw a body on the bed and blood on the floor."

"She's dead?" said McCarthy.

Bowyer nodded.

"Mary Kelly?"

"Yes, it's her. I know her. She's covered in blood."

The two men went back to No. 13. There, John McCarthy looked in the window, using the same method that his employee had.

A few minutes later at nearby Commercial Street Police Station, Inspector Walter Dew of the Criminal Investigation Division or CID, was talking with Inspector Walter Beck, when a man with eyes bulging out of his head and panting for breath rushed into the station.

It was Thomas Bowyer.

"Good God, what is it, man?" Inspector Dew asked him.

"Another one. Jack the Ripper. Awful. Jack McCarthy sent me," came the reply between gasps for breath.

Dew knew local landlord McCarthy. He didn't recognize this fellow, though.

But it didn't matter. He and Inspector Beck were immediately on their feet and on their way to Miller's Court, with as many constables as they could gather from the station.

CHAPTER 29

Like the Work of a Devil

vents now moved with the peculiar rapid slowness which was characteristic of Metropolitan Police investigations. By eleven that morning, the entrance to Miller's Court was blocked off by a constable guarding the Dorset Street end of the passageway. The area around Mary Kelly's corner room at No. 13, Miller's Court was crowded with police constables, three chief constables, two police inspectors, an assistant commissioner, a departmental photographer, and a divisional surgeon.

But curiously, no one had yet ventured inside. Since the door to the room was locked, the divisional surgeon—the same Dr. George Bagster Phillips who had examined the body of the second Ripper victim, Annie Chapman—looked through the window to satisfy himself that no one inside was in need of any immediate medical attention. Then the small law enforcement army on the site decided to wait for two bloodhounds that were said to be on the way. (The information was erroneous.) In the meantime, the window frame was removed so that the police photographer could take several pictures of the gruesome remains on the bed.

At 1.30 p.m., with the news that the bloodhounds weren't coming after all, Superintendent Thomas Arnold ordered that the door to Kelly's room be broken down. John McCarthy, the landlord, carried out this order with a pickaxe.[*]

---

[*] The mystery of the locked door was never solved, since the key was said to have been missing "for some time."

The horror on the bed in Miller's Court could now be examined closely.

As the divisional surgeon for H Division, Dr. Phillips was much closer to the scene of the murder at the time the body was discovered than Scarlet was in his Scotland Yard office in Westminster. By the time Scarlet arrived in Miller's Court—barely twelve hours since he and Pierce-Jones had conducted their surveillance there the previous night—he had also been preceded by Dr. Thomas Bond, who had been reviewing medical evidence in the Ripper murders since October.

Drs. Phillips and Bond were now examining the remains closely, with the latter taking notes. The room was small and crowded with furniture. The extensively mutilated corpse on the bed would have dominated a much larger space. In the claustrophobic confines of No. 13, Miller's Court, it announced its presence with a quiet stillness that was deafening.

The medical particulars of what Scarlet saw on the bed was recorded in Dr. Bond's notes of that afternoon. What one witness described as "like the work of a devil" was described by the physician this way:

> Notes of examination of body of woman found murdered & mutilated in Dorset St.
>
> The body was lying naked in the middle of the bed the shoulders flat, but the axis of the body inclined to the left side of the bed. The head was turned on the left cheek. The left arm was close to the body with the forearm flexed at a right angle & lying across the abdomen, the right arm was slightly abducted from the body & rested on the mattress, the elbow bent & the forearm supine with the fingers clenched. The

legs were wide apart, the left thigh at right angles to the trunk & the right forming an obtuse angle with the pubes.

The whole of the surface of the abdomen & thighs was removed & the abdominal cavity emptied of its viscera. The breasts were cut off, the arms mutilated by several jagged wounds & the face hacked beyond recognition of the features. The tissues of the neck were severed all round down to the bone.

The viscera were found in various parts viz; the uterus & kidneys with one breast under the head, the other breast by the right foot, the liver between the feet, the intestines by the right side & the spleen by the left side of the body.

The flaps removed from the abdomen & thighs were on a table.

The bed clothing at the right corner was saturated with blood, & on the floor beneath was a pool of blood covering about 2 feet square. The wall by the right side of the bed & in a line with the neck was marked by blood which had struck it in a number of separate splashes.

The neck was cut through the skin & other tissue right down to the vertebrae the 5th & 6th being deeply notched. The skin cuts in the front of the neck showed distinct ecchymosis [bruising].

Both breasts were removed by more or less circular incisions, the muscles down to the ribs being attached to the breasts. The intercostals between the 4 5 & 6 ribs were cut through & the contents of the thorax visible through the openings.

The skin & tissues of the abdomen from the costal arch to the pubes were removed in three large flaps.

The Pericardium was open below & the Heart absent.

In the abdominal cavity was some partly digested food of fish & potatoes & similar food was found in the remains of the stomach attached to the intestines.

Scarlet took in the sight of the mutilated corpse on the bed as much as he could at the moment. His mind—not involved in a close clinical examination as those of the other doctors were—rebelled at any further observation and he had to look away. At the same time the thought came, even to his numbed brain, that this was the time to use the unique access he had to this space before it was crowded with others.

Stepping away from the bed, he noticed partially-burned women's clothing in the fireplace, and bent down to get a closer look. Was this clothing Mary Kelly's? Why would the murderer try to destroy the clothing while leaving the gross evidence of his deed on the bed? Then another thought arose which was disturbing yet logical: perhaps the killer had used the light of a fire to carry out his hellish work.

Scarlet was turning back to the room when something caught his eye on the floor next to the fireplace. A pilaster on the right side of the mantel held a mounted rod that swung inward to place a pot over the fire. The rod was pointing out into the room now at perhaps a 60° or 70° angle—exactly where it would be if someone were putting objects into the fireplace and pushing the rod back out of the way. In the corner where the pilaster met the floor, something shiny sat amid the shadows, where it might have been knocked out of a coat pocket by the rod but not noticed in the dark corner. He bent down to see it more closely.

It was a pair of shears of ancient design.

Doctors Phillips and Bond were still examining Mary Jane Kelly's body closely. They didn't see Scarlet pick up the tool and slip it underneath his coat.

The visions flooded his brain.

Scarlet's right hand still held the shears under his coat—and as he touched the object, his powers of *psychometry* took over. He began to experience visions and sounds and scenes connected with the shears. It was happening the same way it had when he'd placed his hands on Anders Haugen's body parts in the morgue.

This time, he saw fire and smelled smoke and burning metal. A pounding filled his ears, and at each blow sparks flew into the air. Then, abruptly, he was in a cave in front of a stone altar, and men in hoods all around him were kneeling at the altar. He was holding the shears as he intoned a chant—an ancient-sounding prayer to summon something or someone(?).

Then, abruptly, he was in this room. It was the early hours of this morning, and the room was lit only by the light of a fire. He was kneeling on the bed and applying pressure with his powerful right arm as he forced the opened shears down the front of Mary Jane Kelly's ample chest and belly, slicing her open. He watched blood flow generously out of the gross wound and spill downwards on both sides of the abdomen, like a river overflowing its banks.

Now time must have caught up to itself, for he heard Dr. Phillips saying:

"What about anatomical knowledge? Do you think he had much?"

"No," Dr. Bond was replying. "None. He would be a man of physical strength and great coolness and daring, certainly. But in my opinion, he does not even possess the technical knowledge of a butcher or horse slaughterer or any person accustomed to cut up dead animals."

The vision had ended.

"Of course," Scarlet said, to himself.

He now knew three things. One: the man who committed this murder *did* have physical strength because he was a blacksmith. Two: he *would* possess coolness and daring, because he was the chief priest of the Friends of the Daughters of Night. Three: he had used *the shears Scarlet was now holding under his coat* to mutilate Mary Jane Kelly in this room eight hours ago.

He also knew the man's name. It was Sidor Zaitsev.

Scarlet could even see Zaitsev's blacksmith's shop in his mind. It was called The White Horse. And it was on Purser's Cross Road, near Parson's Green in the borough of Fulham in southwest London—ten miles or so from where he stood now.

CHAPTER 30

Chase With Beasts in View

carlet knew there was no time to lose. Mary Jane Kelly's murder had taken place in this room approximately eight hours ago. That gave the murderer, Sidor Zaitsev, that many hours to put his plan of escape into action.

Or to die trying.

Surely Zaitsev—the latest of the "Rippers" from the Friends of the Daughters of Night—realized that his own death was a possible outcome of the ritual killing he had just committed. He would have known by now what had happened to the three previous Friends killers.

Perhaps that knowledge might have been enough to stop him from carrying out Mary Jane Kelly's murder in the first place, if religious mania hadn't driven him to disregard his own safety. By now, Scarlet could believe that in Zaitsev's mind, the Friends had a mission, and even the deaths of members who carried out that mission weren't going to stop him.

Drs. Phillips and Bond, the two divisional surgeons who had been assigned the case, were still busy conducting their examination of the victim, Mary Jane Kelly, a few feet away. There was no need for Scarlet to remain on the murder site.

He quietly slipped out of No. 13, Miller's Court and then the courtyard.

He had a new job now—or two new jobs. He must apprehend Zaitsev. At the same time, he had to try to save the man's life.

The Friends of the Daughters of Night had let slip the dogs of war. Whoever was avenging the women's murders that the cult members had committed would be on Zaitsev's trail now. It was up to Scarlet and Pierce-Jones to try and stop them.

The hansom cab ride from Django's house in Mayfair to Fulham took forty minutes. Scarlet had arrived at Pierce-Jones's house barely fifteen minutes earlier. As the cab had waited outside, Scarlet had briefed his friend on what he'd seen in the visions in Mary Jane Kelly's room, and who their quarry was. They both assumed that as the leader of what was essentially a group of religious fanatics, Zaitsev would be dangerous.

They had decided to leave the sacrificial shears in the house in Mayfair, not trusting any power that might be invested in them by Atropos to interfere with their mission. But they intended to be armed when they confronted the Russian émigré Zaitsev. Pierce-Jones had fetched his older model Adams revolver from the drawer in a table by his bedside. Scarlet already had his new standard-issue Webley in his coat pocket.

There was another thought that occupied the minds of the two men as they made their way south-by-southwest in the cab, through Knightsbridge and along the Brompton Road to Fulham Road. They were hoping to save Zaitsev from a violent death, of course. But they were also wondering what it was that they might meet that had already killed three men in the most gruesome of ways.

For they had no idea who or what it was, or how to fight it. So that the revolvers in their pockets gave them no reassurance at all.

Per Scarlet's instructions, the cab rolled to a stop in front of the circulating library on Fulham Road, around the corner from Purser's Cross Road. They would walk to the blacksmith's shop from here.

The clapboard building had a sign which read THE WHITE HORSE, BLACKSMITH SHOP painted in white on its bare wood façade. Someone was hard at work inside, producing the distinctive ring of hammer-on-iron blows that carried to the street outside.

As Scarlet and Pierce-Jones stepped from the daylight into the dark interior, they could see the silhouette of a man's arm rising and falling with perfect precision, like an automaton. With each downward blow, sparks were produced that flew up into the darkness.

The man's arm stopped midway in this movement at the top of its swing. He must have noticed the two of them approaching from the corner of his eye. He turned toward them now. The arm descended slowly from the menacing pose.

"Mr. Zaitsev?" said Scarlet. He and Pierce-Jones had halted a good six feet away.

"Aye."

"I am Dr. William Scarlet, from Scotland Yard. This is my associate, Django Pierce-Jones."

"Tak?"

Scarlet guessed the word to be the equivalent of, "Yes, so?" or something similar in Russian. He was wrong. It was Ukrainian.

"Is there somewhere we could talk? It's rather dark in here."

The man remained perfectly still.

"This is vhere I am vorking," he said, his tone neutral. "I must see color of metal to know right heat. Dat's why dark. You ask me here. Vhat about?"

Scarlet had the impression that that constituted a long speech by the fellow opposite them. Zaitsev had pivoted the upper half of his body toward them, but his feet stayed pointed to the anvil in front of him. He still held the hammer. This attitude announced that he expected the conversation to be brief, and that he intended to get right back to his work.

By the look of him, Sidor Zaitsev might have been born to his job. He was short and bullet-headed, and might be as bald as a bullet as well, for he wore a black cloth cap that was round at the top and tightly fitted on his head down to the ears. His shoulders and arms looked powerful. His hands, face, and neck were of a speckled hue somewhere between gray and black—probably stamped with the labor of decades working with flame and metal. Scarlet thought the name for it was 'Blacksmith's Cast.'

Curiously, the apron Zaitsev wore showed the same effect. It was black from his thighs to his sternum, but graduated back to its original tan where it was far enough from the anvil not to be scorched and blasted by metal being forged. Metal that from its color was at the right heat, of course.

Zaitsev's shaven face might have been clean or dirty at the moment; they couldn't tell. He was squinting at them, revealing massive crow's feet and a single, deep vertical line between his eyes.

"Does the name Evan Whincup mean anything to you?" Scarlet asked.

He had meant the abrupt question to startle the man. But it seemed to have the opposite effect. Zaitsev slowly placed the hammer on a roughly-carved wooden table next to the anvil and turned to face his visitors. He still stood with his feet wide apart, but his hands were now at his side. They looked absurdly large, hanging there.

He started to say something but stopped. He turned his head slightly, his gaze not looking at anything in particular. It was the attitude of someone listening. Scarlet and Django noticed it and listened as well, but they didn't hear anything.

"Is something the matter, sir?" said Scarlet.

But Zaitsev was still listening. Then that look was gone and he was present again.

"Yes, I know dis boy, Evan," he said, answering the question before the last one. "Good boy. He is member of club I belong to."

"You realize he is dead?"

"I know this. He hang himself," Zaitsev replied, and made a quick sign of the cross the Russian Orthodox way, touching his right shoulder first instead of the left.

"Did he say anything to you before he killed himself?" Pierce-Jones asked.

"You policeman too?"

"No, he isn't. He's helping me with my enquiries," Scarlet answered.

"Vhy police ask qvestions about suicide?" asked Zaitsev brusquely. "Not murder."

Scarlet shrugged his shoulders and nodded slightly, conceding the point.

"No, not murder. But we've certainly had enough murders in the East End recently, haven't we? You've heard about them of course?"

Zaitsev didn't answer him.

"What kinds of tools does a blacksmith use?" Scarlet asked, his tone curious.

"Many," said Zaitsev flatly, seemingly undisturbed by the abrupt change of topic.

"What about shears?"

Once again, Scarlet had hoped to catch the other man off guard. But the timing was spoiled, because Zaitsev paused for a good five seconds. Once again he seemed about to answer, then frowned.

"Listen!" he said.

This time they all heard it: the beating of wings. Gigantic wings, somewhere above the roof of the blacksmith's shop.

Then Zaitsev was sprinting with surprising speed through the open barn doors onto Fulham Road. When Scarlet and Pierce-Jones emerged from the shop in pursuit, they saw Zaitsev run across Parsons Green Road, oblivious to the traffic in cabs and horses, and plunge into the trees on the other side of the street. He appeared to be headed for the long greenway that runs along Fulham Road from Parson's Green to Eel Brook Common.

Scarlet and Pierce-Jones raced after him. The greenway was only a sharp point of land at this end; but it gradually grew wider until it opened up into the wide expanse of Eel Brook Common a third of a mile ahead. The Common was huge, as large as ten city blocks.

Once on it, it would be easy for Zaitsev to disappear into the trees, some of which even now in November still had leaves to provide cover.

He ran extraordinarily well. The two of them were going flat-out to keep the same distance behind him, with the taller and younger Pierce-Jones slightly ahead of Scarlet.

The sound they had heard above the roof of the blacksmith's shop seemed to be following them. Unmistakably now, it was the beating of more than one set of wings. But from what . . . and how could wings be this impossibly loud? Were they being followed by eagles or vultures?

With each gap in the trees overhead, the sound of the wings was louder. But there was no time for Scarlet to look up, running as fast as he could after the fleeing figure, but also focusing on the ground in front of him to avoid tripping and falling at full speed.

Then he realized: they weren't being followed.

They were being pursued.

Whatever was up there was *chasing* them.

No, not them.

Zaitsev.

The blacksmith—the chief priest of the Friends of the Daughters of Night and the murderer of Mary Jane Kelly—must know it. He had heard the wings over the shop before Scarlet and Pierce-Jones had. It was why he had chosen the tree-lined greenway, where whatever was flying above them couldn't see him through the leaves.

But a third of a mile is an endless distance when one is running for one's life. From behind, Zaitsev was a different kind of automaton now. His arms and legs pumped in a perfect union of timing and function, and his head rose regularly to scan any opening in the trees' canopy.

Then abruptly the sound of the beating wings was *behind,* not above them. The bottom of the trees' canopy formed a tunnel that the three of them were running through. At some point where there must be a gap, whatever was flying above them had swooped down through the opening and was now coming up behind them.

It was a frightening thought, but before it could register much in Scarlet's mind—and before he had a chance to look over his shoulder—the things had passed closely above his and Pierce-Jones's heads and were between them and Zaitsev.

Now at last he and Django could see them.

There were three of the creatures, and they were flying fast in pursuit of Zaitsev. They were giant and birdlike, but they weren't giant birds. Their feathers were all black, not variegated like the golden eagle, nor with a white head and fantail like the bald eagle. But they were as large as eagles—with a wingspan that must have been six or seven feet.

Like eagles too, they had powerful-looking claws on sturdy legs that were really nothing more than ankles. But their swift passage only feet above Scarlet and Pierce-Jones revealed that they had *human faces*—and long human hair billowed out behind them as they flew swiftly on at great speed.

Up ahead, the terrain was changing. The tunnel-like greenway formed by the trees turned sharply to the left, paralleling Favart Road as it continued northwest. Straight ahead, the greenway became a dirt path that opened abruptly onto the great lawn of Eel Brook Common.

Staying on the greenway to the left meant that one could remain among the trees, and that was the choice Zaitsev made. But he'd made a mistake—unable to see it from here, before the path turned leftward. Following the turn to the left, there was nothing ahead but Novello Road, and beyond that, railroad tracks.

Zaitsev must have realized this just before the plunged onto the leftward path, because he suddenly veered off to the right, where a stand of trees formed a small square. By now, the three birdlike creatures were almost upon him. Scarlet and Django saw all this before they raced onto the same righthand path as the fleeing figure.

By now, their ragged breath came in gasps; but they were unaware of their own breathing as the watched the fantastic chase unfolding in front of them.

They emerged from the trees into a sudden, shocking stillness. Just a few feet in front of them, the path ended and there were two tennis courts which completely filled up the square space formed by the trees. Now, breathing hard, they surveyed the area around them. But they saw neither the blacksmith nor the bird creatures.

How could both Zaitsev and the creatures have vanished within the space of perhaps thirty seconds?

Then they saw that although the court nearest to them was empty, the far court wasn't. Zaitsev was in the middle of that court. He was hunched over, gasping for air and clutching his right side as he faced the net. The three creatures were perched on the net, their broad black birds' backs turned toward Scarlet and Pierce-Jones. They seemed to be just sitting there with their wings folded, looking back at Zaitsev.

Then the wings of the middle creature unfolded slowly. It must have been a signal, because as one the three great bird-humans spread their wings and rose into the air. Zaitsev spun around, ready to run again. But the huge birds were on him before he had time to take the first step, or to scream.

What Scarlet and Django saw then was a chaotic rising and plunging back down of giant black forms, the powerful movements of huge wings, and claws that sunk in and pulled back again and again, tossing what looked like long red ribbons into the air. By the time the birds finished and rose up higher, the once-green tennis court had turned red. Aligning themselves perfectly in the sky, they beat their wings powerfully to quickly cover the short distance between the scene of their savagery and the place where Scarlet and Django stood observing them.

They landed on the branches of a beech tree no more than thirty feet from where the two men stood. Then they used their wings to flutter gently to the ground. They were close enough that Scarlet and Django couldn't have been mistaken at what they were looking at now, however inexplicable it was.

Three women—not young, not old—stood looking back at them from where the bird creatures had been seconds earlier. The women had wild dark eyes and stringy unkempt hair and claw-like human hands that held together coarse-cut garments across their chests. But they were *women*, not birdlike creatures. They did not speak, but stood regarding the men with a mixture of agelessness and curiosity. There was malevolence in them, the men knew, but it was a dark power not aimed in their direction.

Then they were gone, and Scarlet and Pierce-Jones could breathe again.

They didn't wonder how the transformation or disappearance had come about.

They didn't care.

CHAPTER 31

Goddesses of Vengeance

s far as the public, the police, and the press were concerned, Mary Jane Kelly was the last of "Jack the Ripper's" victims. There had been five: Mary Ann Nichols, Annie Chapman, Elizabeth Stride, Catherine Eddowes, and Mary Kelly. The people, the authorities, and the newspapers knew nothing of the fact that four men who had been found brutally dismembered had also perished as a result of these murders: Anders Haugen, George Ross, Chas Widdington, and Sidor Zaitsev.

Though two more prostitutes were murdered in Whitechapel during the next two and a half years, neither case was similar to the earlier killings. As far as Scotland Yard was concerned, the Jack the Ripper investigation, though still officially open, was over. The identity of—in their minds—the man who had terrorized London for three months, from August to November of 1888, remained unknown.

Only the Society for Supernatural and Psychic Research's file on the case was truly closed. Its members William Scarlet and Django Pierce-Jones knew how and why the five unfortunate women of the East End were murdered—and how those women were avenged by the savage deaths of the four men who had killed them.

Even years later, the two of them would sometimes wonder—

in their individual dark moments when they questioned the reality of the world around them—if they had seen and experienced the wonders that they had during that time. But this history of events in London in the summer and fall of a fateful year begins and ends there. It doesn't ask anything, as Scrooge did, of a ghost from the future.

Here it is still November 1888, the 23rd of the month—a Friday evening exactly two weeks after the murder of Mary Kelly. Scarlet and Pierce-Jones are having drinks before dinner at the latter's house in Mayfair. It has taken this long for the two of them to be able to talk about what they saw on Eel Brook Common in Fulham a fortnight ago. And to put together all the pieces of what is, essentially, an ancient puzzle.

Scarlet has completed his research (he has not asked Bilby this time), and thinks he understands the meaning of the events. He hardly dares speak of it, however, even to his friend, Django Pierce-Jones, who is generally more conversant with the occult than he is. The words he uses now show why.

"This entire case is quite beyond reason," Scarlet states flatly. "If anyone were to tell it to me—including Bilby—I'd say they were mad."

His gaze rests on the ancient shears on the coffee table in front of them.

"Just look at those: an archaic, ancient design that probably hasn't been seen in centuries. Yet here they are, as tangible as anything else in this room."

"And more deadly," adds Pierce-Jones.

"Yes, of course," Scarlet agrees. "An ancient weapon of death, provided by a Greek goddess summoned into the present by a group of modern worshippers. Who would believe such a thing?"

He shakes his head, and continues.

"But consider it, Django. We formed the Society to study occult occurrences that couldn't be explained otherwise. Who'd have thought our investigations would find us in the midst of something like this? A group of working men who took it upon themselves to cleanse society of what they considered evil. They had no idea of the forces they were unleashing."

And then he asks:

"Do you know the story of the Fates?"

"Broadly," Django answers. "They aren't something you expect to encounter in nineteenth-century London. Or at least, they weren't."

Scarlet grins. "There are more things in heaven and earth, Horatio, than are dreamt of in your philosophy," he quotes in reply.

"There were three Fates, or Moirai: Clotho, 'The Spinner,' who spun the thread of life on a great loom. Lachesis was 'The Drawer of Lots,' who measured the length of the thread, which was the person's lifespan. The third one, Atropos, 'The Unyielding,' was the goddess that the Friends of the Daughters of Night summoned. She was the Fate who cut the thread of life at the apportioned length, meaning at the appointed time."

"With those," says Django, pointing to the shears on the coffee table. "But why 'The Friends of the Daughters of Night'? What was the significance of the name of the organization that the four murderers—Haugen, Ross, Widdington, and Zaitsev—belonged to?"

Scarlet reaches over to refresh both of their drinks.

It is an excellent whisky.

"That's the great irony of the story. The club chose the name of another trio of goddesses from ancient mythology who would in fact destroy them. There were three of them as well: Allecto or 'Unceasing in Anger,' Tisiphone, 'The Avenger of Murder,' and Megaera, 'The Jealous.' They were the daughters of Darkness and Gaea, the Earth Mother, and so, the daughters of night.

"The Greeks called them Erinyes, or Eumenides, a name meaning 'kindly'. Evidently, these three goddesses were so savage that people were afraid to say their real name out loud. We have another name for them: The Furies."

"And the Friends of the Daughters of Night never counted on these goddesses coming after them."

"They should have," Scarlet replies, his tone deadly serious. "That's what they do. The Furies are the goddesses of vengeance. They are deities of the underworld whose role is to ascend to Earth to pursue and punish the wicked—especially murderers of the innocent.

"You see, the women the London Friends killed were prostitutes . . ."

"But these 'unfortunates' were just that, and were innocent of shedding any blood themselves," Django finishes the thought.

"That's exactly right—and that's a good way to put it," says Scarlet. He reflects for a moment. "But now, we possess Atropos's divine weapon, as the Friends thought of it, that allowed them to carry out their murders."

"Will they try again?"

"I doubt it. Their leader is dead, and the consequences of their actions must be clear to them. I imagine it's the end of this short reign of terror in Whitechapel."

"But what about these two groups of goddesses who ended up on opposing sides—the Fates and the Furies? Are they fighting each other now in London?"

"No, I don't think so," answers Scarlet. "The Furies were simply carrying out their ancient role, as they are bound to do. They were chasing down murderers. There's no reason for them to confront the Fate named Atropos, who in her own mind was carrying out her duties as well. Unfortunately, the mortals who lost their lives got caught between the conflicting roles of these ancient deities, and suffered."

"Just as usually happened in Greek mythology," says Django.

"That's true. The way it's always been, you might say."

"Which is why the Furies had no interest in killing us on Eel Brook Common."

"Thank God," adds Scarlet.

But Django shakes his head.

"Or all of them," he corrects his friend.

Keep reading after "Notes and Sources" for a preview of
Book #3 in the
Dr. William Scarlet Mysteries — *The Master of Illusion*

NOTES AND SOURCES

The Jack the Ripper murders are, of course, factual. Yet hundreds of novels, short stories, periodicals, songs, plays, and entertainments have been imagined using the actual events as a starting place.

Year of the Rippers is one of those fictions.

The public domain historical records, secondary sources, and online sites I have consulted in my research are cited in footnotes below. The actions of the Fates or Moirai, and the Furies (Greek Erinyes or Eumenides), both from Greek mythology, are my own invention.

I have also taken the liberty of changing dates slightly where it suits the story.

A note concerning language: In Victorian England, it was common to refer to physicians as "*Mr.* So-and-So," though "Dr." was also used. The use of both "Mr. Scarlet" and "Dr. Scarlet," sometimes by the same character, is intentional.

Prologue

Divisional Reference H302: Metropolitan Police report, H Division, 8 September 1888. Included in Stewart P. Evans and Keith Skinner, *The Ultimate Jack the Ripper Sourcebook* (London: Constable & Robinson, 2001), 55-56 (Kindle edition). Note: the author was unable to locate the original of this document, as the

National Archives of the UK, England, and Wales stated in response to my inquiry: "This item does not contain material earlier than 10 Sept 1888." Email from National Archives Record Copying to the author, 22 May 2023.

sometimes known as "Siffey," "Sivvey," or "Sievey": https://www.victorianwhitechapel.tumblr.com/Annie-Chapman

Chapter 1

People of the Abyss: Jack London, *The People of the Abyss* (1903).

fur pullers: https://victorianlondon.substack.com/p/fur-pullers.

cost of a doss house and cooking in the kitchen: Patricia Cornwell, *Portrait of a Killer: Jack the Ripper Case Closed* (New York: G.P. Putnam's Sons, 2002): 79.

numbers of prostitutes, brothels, and doss houses; St George in the East: Bruce Paley, *Jack the Ripper: The Simple Truth* (London: Headline Book Publishing, 1996): 20-28.

one of every five children: https://www.bbc.co.uk/history/british/victorians/overview_victorians_01.shtml.

Chapter 2

Wilmott's, 18 Thrawl Street: https://www.jack-the-ripper.org/life-and-death-of-mary-nichols.htm.

"I'll get my doss money" and jolly bonnet: T.M. Thorne, *The Ripper Reports: Jack the Ripper and the Whitechapel Murders as Reported by the Victorian* Press (T.M. Thorne, 2021): 40 (Kindle edition).

straw bonnet trimmed with black velvet:
https://www.allthatsinteresting.com/mary-ann-nichols.
The worn description of the bonnet is my own.

around 2.30 . . . last reported sighting:
https://www.wiki.casebook.org/emily_holland.html.

Cross and the tarpaulin, and crime scene description: Nichols inquest, report of Inspector Frederick Abberline of 19 September 1888, MEPO 3/140, ff. 242-3, and the newspapers *Star, Daily Telegraph, Daily News, The Times,* and *East London Advertiser.* Reported in Philip Sugden, *The Complete History of Jack the Ripper* (New York: Carroll & Graf, 1994): 36-42.

not more than would fill two wine glasses: Sugden, 39.

bowels protruded: Thorne, 30.

the victim was five feet two . . . Lambeth Workhouse: Donald Rumbelow, *Jack the Ripper: The Complete Casebook* (Chicago/New York: Contemporary Books, 1988): 40-41.

Chapter 4

origin of Chislehurst caves and denehole: Rev. J. W. Hayes, "Deneholes and Other Chalk Excavations: Their Origins and Uses," *Journal of the Royal Anthropological Institute of Great Britain and Ireland* (1909): 44, 54–55. Accessed at
https://archive.org/details/v38a39journalofro38royauoft/page/54/mode/2up?view=theater.

chthonic worship: Stewart Brekke, "Ouranic and Chthonic Deities and Rituals". *Classical Bulletin* 67 (1991): 33, via ProQuest. Accessed on Wikipedia: "Chthonic."

dry ice: British Army Medical Corps doctor Herbert Samuel Elworthy was actually granted a patent to solidify carbon dioxide in 1897. Here, I have anticipated his invention by nine years. https://dryiceinfo.com/history/.

weaving goddesses: https://www.greekmythology.com/Other_Gods/The_Fates/the_fat es.html.

children of Nyx: https://www.theoi.com/Protogenos/Nyx.html.

The Unturning: https://mythologysource.com/three fates.

Chapter 5

time of Annie Chapman's death: https://inews.co.uk/culture/television/jack-the-ripper-victims-whitechapel-murders-who-women-killed-276601.

Richardson's schedule:; Testimony of John Richardson at Chapman Inquest. Reported in *The Times,* 13 September 1888. Evans and Skinner, 86-87.

cat's meat shop, six families: *Eastern Evening News,* 10 September 1888. Quoted in Thorne, 59-60.

a lunatic of this sort: *Tower Hamlets Independent* and *East End Local Advertiser*, 8 September 1888, Thorne, 52.

Chapter 7

30,000 physicians: An educated guess concerning 1888. Actual numbers are not available for all years. In 1861, there were 14,415 physicians in England and Wales, and 22,698 in 1901. However, the General Medical Council register shows 35,650 names at the turn of the century, including 6,580 serving in the military or imperial service.

http://www.vam.ac.uk/content/articles/h/health-and-medicine-in-the-19th-century/.

Chapter 8

Jack the Ripper letter: https://whitechapeljack.com/the-ripper-letters/.

Chapter 9

a dull and cloudy day: "Weather Conditions for the Nights of the Whitechapel Murders," courtesy of Casebook Productions. https://casebook.org/victorian_london/weather.html.

she was dressed in a cheap black dress: *Daily Chronicle,* 1 October 1888, quoted in Paley, 81.

on the cottages opposite: *Shields Daily Gazette,* 1 October 1888, Thorne, 107.

timing of movements in Dutfield's Yard: Depositions of Morris Eagle and Louis Diemschutz, 1 October 1888, in *Daily Telegraph, Daily* News, and *The Times,* 2 October 1888. See Sugden, 166-168.

testimony of PC Smith, Israel Schwartz, and William Marshall: *The*

Times, 6 October 1888, 6. Reported in Evans and Skinner, 136-137, 184-185.

"Lipski" as a term of insult to Jews: Israel Lipski was an East European Jew executed the previous year for murder. https://www.timesofisrael.com/were-the-jack-the-ripper-murders-an-elaborate-anti-semitic-frameup/.

dimensions of Mitre Square: Thorne, 103.

deserted and in almost complete darkness: https://www.jack-the-ripper-tour.com/generalnews/mitre-square-through-time/.

PC Richard Pearce lived there: https://forum.casebook.org/forum/ripper-discussions/police-officials-and-procedures/general-police-discussion/11093-pc-richard-pearce-and-the-candle-in-the-window.

description and chronology of police patrols in Mitre Square: Paley, 97. Paley places PC Watkins's return to Mitre Square at 1.46 a.m. Sugden uses 1.44 a.m., while Thorne cites the *Shields Daily Gazette*'s "a quarter to two o'clock." The report of Inspector James McWilliam to the City Police of 27 October 1888 states: "On the 30th September at 1.45 a.m. a woman since identified as Catherine Eddowes was found with her throat cut & disembowelled in Mitre Square." I have used the 1.45 time specified by McWilliam in his official report.

Morris statement: *Lloyds Newspaper*, 7 October 1888. Cited in Paley, 97.

Description of Catherine Eddowes's clothing and background: Corporation of London Records Office, Coroner's Inquests (L), 1888, No. 135. Also, *Daily Telegraph* and *The Times*, 1 October

1888. In Sugden, 231-232.

Don't you fear for me: https://whitechapeljack.com/the-whitechapel-murders/catherine-eddowes-aka-kate-conway-aka-kate-kelly/.

Too late to get any more drink (conversation between PC George Hutt and Eddowes): https://www.jack-the-ripper.org/kate-eddowes-last-night.htm.

Eddowes autopsy: Ref. Coroner's Inquest (L), 1888, No. 135, Catherine Eddowes inquest, 1888 (Corporation of London Record Office). Cited in Evans and Skinner, 228-230.

She was ripped up: Quote from PC Edward Watkins. Cited in https://acidhistory.wordpress.com/2012/04/29/the-victims-of-jack-the-ripper/.

in a space that measured only eighteen feet: https://red-jack.blogspot.com/2013/09/berner-street-dutfields-yard.html.

at the very time that Dr. Brown: Cornwell, 238.

activity on Berner Street and Mitre Square, and Matthews and Warren called upon to resign: *Pall Mall Gazette,* 1 October 1888. See Thorne, 117-119.

Chapter 11

Norwegian language: https://www.lifeinnorway.net/norwegian-phrases/.

Chapter 12

£1 9s: Cornwell, 344.

kind enough to invite fellow prostitutes, and Barnett reading to Kelly: https://forum.casebook.org/forum/ripper-discussions/victims/mary-jane-kelly/766835-barnett-the-indefinite-article.

"She was one of the most decent . . . quarrelsome and abusive": *Yorkshire Post,* 12 November 1888, quoting Elizabeth Phoenix. Cited in Paul Begg, *Jack the Ripper: The Uncensored Facts* (London: Robson Books, 1990): 144.

Chapter 15

the Spinner: https//mythologysource.comabusive/three-fates/.

Chapter 16

Thames Street was famous: https://www.victorianlondon.org/shops/bazaars.htm.

caddy spoons: Alexa MacDermot, "10 Ingenious Cutlery Inventions from the Victorian Era," https://listverse.com/2018/08/28/10-ingenious-cutlery-inventions-from-the-victorian-era/.

Egyptian and Roman shears: https://www.backthenhistory.com/articles/the-history-of-styling-shears.

Chapter 17

the good reader makes the good book: Ralph Waldo Emerson, *Society and Solitude* (1870).

Chapter 18

tosher: https://www.familysearch.org/en/wiki/Victorian_England_Occupations_in_City_and_Town.

evidence of suicidal hanging: Dinesh Rao, "An autopsy study of death due to Suicidal Hanging – 264 cases," in *Egyptian Journal of Forensic Sciences* Volume 6, Issue 3, September 2016, Pages 248-254, accessed at https://www.sciencedirect.com/science/article/pii/S2090536X1500 0052.

Also, https://www.barnardhealth.us/forensic-pathology/external-examination-of-hanging-deaths.html.

Chapter 19

"We are inundated with suggestions and names of suspects": Police letter, 9 October 1888 from Charles Warren to Sir James Fraser. MEPO 1/48.

https://cdn.nationalarchives.gov.uk/documents/education/jackther ipper.pdf. I have changed the date of this actual letter from October 9 to November 4. The crumpling and retrieval of the paper are invented.

Chapter 20

kidneys not injured by alcohol: Sugden, 273.

American hat and certain observations: Thorne, 133-134.

person in Vienna: Evans and Skinner, 347.

Godless brutality: *The Times*, 18 September 1888; London has not been indifferent: *Morning Advertiser*, 19 September; Whitechapel Horrors: *The Times*, 19 September. All three sources cited in Paley, 125-126.
vigilance committees: Sugden, 123-124.

Chapter 21

Dannemann cigars: https://en.wikipedia.org/wiki/Dannemann.

Chapter 22

"darkest London": "Victorian Houses and Where Victorians Lived," https://victorianchildren.org/victorian-houses-how-victorians-lived/.

Chapter 24

she made Joe read the newspaper stories to her: Inquest, *The Standard*, 13 November 1888, cited in Paley, 42.

her rent of 4 shillings a week: Evans and Skinner, 371.

she decided to visit Elizabeth Prater: https://wiki.casebook.org/elizabeth_prater.html.

the Lord Mayor's Show: Sugden, 310-311.

Horn of Plenty pub: Paley, 145.

immoral courses: "Another Whitechapel Atrocity, Murder and Mutilation of a Woman This Morning, Special Descriptive Account, The Head Severed From the Body, Ghastly Sight," *Manchester Evening News*, 9 November 1888. Cited in Thorne, 247.

George Hutchinson and description of customer: Metropolitan Police Files, 3/140, ff. 227-9, as quoted in Evans and Skinner, 418-419.

Chapter 28

Mary Ann Cox and description of Kelly singing: Inquest testimony and statement by Mary Ann Cox to Inspector Abberline. MJ/SPC/NE 1888. Box 3, No. 19. Greater London Archives, Coroner's papers. Cited in Begg, 152-153.

a pensioned soldier: *St James's Gazette,* 10 November 1888; *Daily Telegraph,* 10 November 1888, cited in "Thomas Bowyer," https://wiki.casebook.org/thomas_bowyer.html.

"I knocked at the door" and Bowyer's statements: Inquest, *Daily Telegraph*, 13 November 1888. Quoted in Paley, 148.

eyes bulging out of his head: *I Caught Crippen: Memoirs of Ex-Chief Inspector Walter Dew CID*, Walter Dew (Blackie and Son 1938), cited in https://wiki.casebook.org/thomas_bowyer.html.

Chapter 29

description of the police presence and actions at the scene of the Kelly murder: Paley, 148-151.

like the work of a devil: https://www.jack-the-ripper.org/mary-kelly-murder.htm.

Dr. Bond's "Notes of examination of body of woman" (Mary Jane Kelly post-mortem examination): Ref. MEPO 3/3153, ff. 10-18, as quoted in Evans and Skinner, 382-384.

anatomical knowledge and dialogue: Bond, 10 November 1888, to Anderson, HO 144/221/A49301C/21 and MEPO 3/140 ff. 220-3, cited in Sugden, 320.

Chapter 31

three Moirai: https://mythologysource.com/three-fates/.

Erinyes: Adam Augustyn, "Furies," in *The Encyclopaedia Britannica*, https://www.britannica.com/topic/Furies.

Following is a preview of *The Master of Illusion* —
Book #3 in the Dr. William Scarlet Mysteries

PROLOGUE

The sound was sharp, like something pointed striking wood.

From his position at the back of the nave in St Michael and All the Angels Church, the Rev. Charles Hathersley thought it came from the other end of the church near the altar. It was hard to say, though, because the twelfth-century building was notorious for echoing and magnifying every sound.

He listened, and heard it again. Yes, it seemed to come from just beyond the three-pointed Gothic arch that separated the nave from the altar. Was someone walking there?

The church was pitch black at 3.25 a.m.—the hour between three and four when the soul is most vulnerable and those who are weak die, thought the Reverend—for he hadn't bothered to turn on any of the gas lamps. He had been thinking that the dark was suited to his thoughts. But now he wished that something more than starlight were filtering through the arched side windows into the central space of the church.

Rev. Hathersley was afraid. Of an unrecognized sound in the dark, yes. But of something bigger than that, something he thought was coming. It was the reason he was up at this time of night or early morning, roaming the halls of the dark church like a ghost. Or scurrying like prey.

"By heaven, it won't help to think like *that*, Charlie," he told himself as he took his first steps down the center aisle toward the altar.

His fear had been hardly noticeable at first, a small cloud

drifting across the sun. Then, over the course of just two weeks, it had grown into something that seemed to take all the light from the world. So that now in this darkness, it was at its strongest, weighing his shoulders down as he walked with a heavy sense of dread.

The interior of St Michael's was all diagonal ribs carved from dark wood and stone pillars and arches, and now it was his own footsteps that echoed throughout the nave due to these natural acoustical materials. A newer church made of brick—he had seen them—would deaden sounds so that there wasn't this confusing echo. That would make things easier for him. But he knew that the way of an Anglican vicar is never meant to be easy.

His enemy wasn't a mystery to Rev. Hathersley—hadn't been even at the start two weeks ago, when he first realized he was in jeopardy. But this darkness put him too much at a disadvantage.

He would light some candles as soon as he reached the altar.

Approaching the front of the church with the pulpit on his left and the hymn board on his right, he could see the altar now. The fair linen cloth always present between services that included Holy Communion was there, as was the plain wooden cross, and the two tall gold candlesticks with candles at either end. In St Michael and All the Angels Church, the entire wall behind the altar was of stained glass, shaped in the form of the Gothic arches which led to it. So there was no room for the larger cross which some churches placed there.

As he walked past the last of the dark wood pews, ready to ascend the two steps to the altar to light the candles, something to his left caught his eye. It was on the wall nearest to and beyond the pulpit.

He turned his head to look. When he saw what he did, logic compelled him to admit that either interior wall—to the left and right of the altar—were the only places where this could have been put.

It was at that moment that Rev. Charles Hathersley understood the fate that was in store for him.

The sharp sound he'd heard earlier came once more. This time, however, it was from directly behind him.

CHAPTER 1

London Is Itself Again

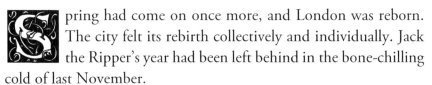pring had come on once more, and London was reborn. The city felt its rebirth collectively and individually. Jack the Ripper's year had been left behind in the bone-chilling cold of last November.

You felt coldest, thought William Scarlet as he watched the swans and ducks in the Hyde Park Serpentine, not in winter, but in late autumn, when you've dressed too lightly to be out all day. Last summer and fall, it was as if London had been like that day after day, powerless against an inescapable cold fear that crept into its bones and stayed there.

But now the warm March sun was shining and, cruel as it may be, it was pleasant to think that the horror of last year was a thing of the past. That certainly wasn't true concerning the tidal wave of articles, pamphlets, speeches, and books that had deluged London since the Ripper murders and which, Scarlet was sure, would continue for some time to come. But he thought that it was probably true, at least, in the minds of the people of London whose lives were already burdened by a daily struggle to survive.

Of course, the world would never know the truth about the five women who were murdered and carved up in awful fashion in Whitechapel, Spitalfields, and The City from August to November of last year. As far as London and the rest of the country were concerned, someone self-named "Jack the Ripper" had committed the crimes: a monster who had never been caught.

Only Scarlet and his friend Django Pierce-Jones knew about the vigilante group—the Friends of the Daughters of Night—that had really committed the murders of Mary Ann Nichols, Annie Chapman, Elizabeth Stride, Catherine Eddowes, and Mary Jane Kelly. And how each of the murderers had in turn suffered a savage retribution for their crimes.*

One day, perhaps, everyone else would know as well. That is, if The Society for Supernatural and Psychic Research that Scarlet and Pierce-Jones belonged to ever decided to open their files to the public .

At any rate, it wasn't Scarlet's concern.

Right now, the unseasonably warm March temperature and the springtime breezes were fine enough to crowd out the somber thoughts from a few months past. They made the blood race through Scarlet's veins, it seemed, for the first time in months.

"Wake up, doctor."

Scarlet looked up, but he was at a complete disadvantage. Whoever the woman was, she was standing between the sun and the bench he was sitting on, so he was looking up at nothing but a female silhouette. He leaned slightly to the left, and began to smile and stand at the same time.

"Miss Wilson. What an unexpected pleasure!"

"Are you sure you don't mean 'distraction,' Dr. Scarlet?" She wore a slightly mocking smile as they shook hands.

She was as striking as he remembered: a tall woman whose features immediately advertised both her attractiveness and intelligence. He remembered now her flawless rose complexion and naturally wavy auburn hair, which she still wore past her shoulders. Her eyes were just as large and dark, her eyebrows thin and arched

---

* See Book 2 in the Dr. William Scarlet mystery series, *Year of the Rippers* (Cedar & Maitland Press, 2024).

in the same way she had trimmed them previously. If her nose remained slightly long, he didn't mind, for her generously wide mouth once again made the proportions pleasing.

This was Catherine Wilson. She was the older sister of Elizabeth Wilson, whose fiancé at the time, Ambrose Reed, had been the target of a dangerous demonic possession which Scarlet had helped uncover and defeat a year and a half ago. Reed had recovered well, and from everything Scarlet had heard since then, had reclaimed his position as London's hottest young painter.

Scarlet guessed Catherine's age at a year or so less than his own thirty-four—unusual for a not-yet-married woman in English society. He put it down to her intelligence and boldness of personality. Together, they probably scared away the not remotely equal suitors that would be available to her.

He released his hand from her firm grip and indicated the now-empty bench.

"Please," he said, adding: "That is, do you have a moment?"

She had on a full-length velvet-like hooped skirt in what Scarlet would call a rich Russian Blue; a black ladies jacket that came to three-quarters length on her arms; and black ankle boots. Had the weather been colder, she probably would have been carrying a muff the same color as the jacket, and a bonnet of some kind, though now her head was bare.

It was a simple and elegant outfit, and he noted it in particular because of the way Catherine Wilson sat down while wearing it. She did it the way women of breeding manage it—moving effortlessly from the standing position to the sitting one while remaining straight as a ramrod the entire time. She took a deep breath, closed her eyes and turned her face to the sun.

"'Daffodils, that come before the swallow dares, and take the winds of March with beauty.'"

"Shakespeare, *The Winter's Tale*."

"Very good, Doctor!" she said, lowering her head to look at him where he sat beside her.

"Even though there's no wind today."

"Well, there's that," said Catherine Wilson, laughing.

"You're looking wonderful, madam," he said, hoping that he sounded as sincere as he was. "If anything, younger by a year or two since I last saw you. How do you manage it, Miss Wilson?"

"If anything, sir, addressing me as 'madam,' and 'Miss Wilson,' makes me sound ancient! I insist you call me Catherine . . . that is, if I may address you as William?"

"You may. All right, Catherine. But my question remains: how do you manage it?"

"It's all illusion, William. I mostly employ angles and mirrors to my benefit."

"What? Out in the open like this?"

"Ah! You're obviously not used to seeing a master at work, sir."

He bowed his head, placing his hand on his breast. "I concede the point." He smiled. "And how are your sister and her husband?"

"Deliriously happy. Mr. and Mrs. Reed are expecting, you see."

"That's marvelous!" said Scarlet, who hadn't heard the news.

"I assure you they are both quite wonderful," said Catherine. "Thanks to you."

Scarlet responded as one does to such a statement. He lowered his head slightly, smiled a tight smile, and said nothing.

"And what about you? Your practice, and your work at Scotland Yard. Are they going well?"

"They are. We're as busy as ever, you may be sure."

There was no need to mention the fallout from the Ripper investigation of last year, which consumed not only the Metropolitan Police/Scotland Yard, but the City of London force as well, and continued to be a black eye for the Home Office. And of course, he could never share the truth about the murders which his own investigation and that of Pierce-Jones had uncovered.

Turning their bodies slightly toward one another on the bench, the two exchanged the polite inquiries which are part of a chance meeting like this one:

- How are your parents? [This referred to Mr. Hiram Wilson, Head of the Railway Department, and his wife Margaret.]

- And your good friend, that dashing gentleman, Django Pierce-Jones?

- My time? Well, I'm teaching a course as demonstrator of anatomy at St George's Hospital. Yes, I'm enjoying it immensely. . . . Are you enjoying the start of the Season?

- Oh, yes. And you? Have you attended the dance or the theatre? (She didn't think he was the opera type, so she didn't include it.)

"Have you seen the latest sensation?" she asked now.

He looked at her blankly. He hadn't a clue of what she meant.

"I'm afraid not. What is the latest sensation?"

"The magicians, of course. And the fierce rivalry between the two greatest of them!"

Scarlet shook his head while shrugging his shoulders. Catherine Wilson took his meaning immediately.

"You *are* spending too much time in your anatomy room, or whatever it's called," she scolded him. "Don't you know that this is the season of magic in London? It's simply everywhere." Her tone had a mocking quality.

"Sorry," he said, though he wasn't. "I must have missed it."

"You certainly appear to have done so! If you had read the society columns, you'd know that it began last year. There's been considerable interest here and on the continent in spiritualism because of the stage shows of the Fox Sisters and the Davenport Brothers in America. Spirit cabinets and all of that. . . . Surely you've heard of the spiritualist movement?"

"Of course," he replied. And he had. He simply hadn't had the time to follow any of it closely. Anyway, Pierce-Jones, who was a true medium, would be much more familiar with the phenomenon than he was.

"Then you must know that a few years ago, stage magicians began exposing the trickery involved in the spiritualist performances. Well, who better?"

"What's the difference, then?"

"You mean between the spiritualism shows and the magicians?"

"Exactly."

"Well, as I understand it, magicians always claim that their illusions are 'honest'—that they use conjuring tricks purely for entertainment. Magic for magic's sake, as it were. They say it's only the frauds who claim to have true spiritual powers. And it appears to be working. The spiritualist movement is on the wane. People seem to like the fact that magic tricks are all illusion. They know it's impossible, yet want it to happen right in front of their eyes every night."

"And this has created a craze in the London theatres?"

"Not in the theatres—in the music halls and on the variety stages. That, and the rivalries that have sprung up as to which magician features the best act. Some of the stage effects have become quite elaborate. People are now going from one music hall to another, to see which magician has outdone the other with the latest grand illusion.

"Do you see, then," she concluded in the same matter-of-fact tone, "how your dedication to the advancement of science has made you miss out on this stupendous turn of events?" She picked up on his own earlier thought and said: "I'll bet your friend, Mr. Pierce-Jones, knows all about it, and has probably seen some of it."

"No doubt. What is the rivalry between the two greatest magicians that you mentioned?"

"Oh. There's a very public competition going on between Max von Leiden, who is known as 'The Master of Illusion,' and Giuseppe Caliosto, who calls himself 'Marco the Magnificent.'"

"I must say, it sounds like an earth-shattering battle."

"You may mock, Doctor, but the season is abuzz with the tit-for-tat performances by the two of them. In fact, these two gentlemen attract enough crowds that they are regularly booked into the theatres rather than the music halls. Herr Von Leiden is currently enjoying an eight-week run at the Queen Victoria Theatre

Royal, and Signor Caliosto recently opened a gala show at Covent Garden."

Scarlet knew that those two theatres were, in fact, major venues.

"Live and learn," he admitted defeat. "It appears you're right . . . I have been missing out. Thank you for—"

"Bringing you back from the dead?" Catherine Wilson said before he could finish, and stood.

Scarlet laughed.

"As to that, I refuse to comment," he said, rising in his turn.

They shook hands once more, this time in departure.

CHAPTER 2

A Stupendous World of Magic

t is remarkably easy for a medical doctor to spend all of his time with sick and injured people, in discussions with colleagues, and attending to patients in hospital. For a police surgeon, the autopsy suite in the sub-basement of Scotland Yard at 5, Whitehall Place, Westminster was simply another version of the same Venus Fly Trap.

Scarlet had been thinking along these lines since his conversation with Catherine Wilson in Hyde Park.

Back from the dead, indeed.

It was springtime, and a pair of shows performed by rival master magicians seemed in order. No, more than in order—absolutely necessary!

Scarlet had been interested in amateur theatrics his whole life, and had performed in the school dramatic clubs at Enfield Academy in North London and at Balliol College, Oxford. One day from that time still stood out vividly in his memory. It was an outing with some friends from the academy and three girls from the neighboring country girls' school who had been drafted for the boys' school's play.

The group had come upon a fair, set up on nearby Bentley Heath. Seeing it, one of the girls had remarked: "A fair was the last thing I expected to find today. But now, attending one is the only thing in the world I want to do!"

Scarlet had been struck by the remark that day, and it had stayed with him. It seemed to sum up the actor's personality: the ability to immerse oneself wholly in an imaginary world at the drop of a hat—and the more fantastical that world, the better.

It was how he felt now about attending a magic show. There would be criminal cases and autopsies enough tomorrow and the day after that. In the meantime, he felt that his soul needed to breathe, as much as his lungs hungered for the spring air after winter.

His morning sessions with patients at the surgery in his home in Chelsea were finished, and his administrative load wasn't burdensome at the moment. He could leave Whitehall, return home to change, and meet Django Pierce-Jones for dinner at Scarlet's club, the Athenaeum at 8.00 as planned.

"I want you to tell me about the magicians' shows currently in London," he said to Pierce-Jones after they'd shaken hands and sat down in the Athenaeum's dining room. "And whatever you know about the spiritualists' shows."

Django look at his friend steadily.

He said: "I was thinking of the sole. Or . . ." (a quick look back at the menu) "perhaps the leg of lamb. What do you suggest?"

"All right, bastard," replied Scarlet with a grin. "Sorry. Let's order."

The food was always exceptional at the Athenaeum, and Pierce-Jones probably would have preferred to sample more of it before he finally replied to Scarlet's comments of the last few minutes.

"Catherine's absolutely right," he said. "Tickets to the magic shows are the hottest items in London right now. Especially those of von Leiden and Caliosto, who have developed quite a rivalry."

"So I understand," said Scarlet. "And what's so special about these two?"

Pierce-Jones smiled, took a sip of Brunello di Montalcino,* and leaned back in his forest-green tufted dining chair.

"They are the greatest of the greatest—the *crème de la crème*—at least in their own minds. Truth be told, they are both spectacular magicians. They recently developed a rivalry that has each of them trying to over-top the other in remarkable illusions, sometimes on the same night. It's a wonder they're not blasting each other with magic wands from opposite street corners in the theatre district. Fortunately, one of them performs at the Queen Victoria Theatre Royal in Haymarket, and the other in Covent Garden."

"That's only a half-mile's distance from each other."

"Well, it's a sight better than if Caliosto weren't at Covent Garden but at Her Majesty's Theatre, which is just across the damned street from the Theatre Royal where von Leiden is appearing."

It always amused Scarlet to hear Pierce-Jones employ a British gentleman's expressions. 'Damned street,' indeed!

Scarlet wasn't convinced. "Mightn't a famous public rivalry be just another trick to fill the house?"

"I don't think so," replied Django. "I believe it's personal. There have been comments, for instance, that have revealed considerable animosity."

"Fair enough," said Scarlet, tucking into his food again. "Tell me about these two great magicians."

"Well, you know that practically every magician uses 'Famous,' 'Extraordinary,' 'Amazing,' and so on before their name, right?"

"Of course."

"And someone is always declaring he has 'The World's Greatest

---

* A red wine from the hill town of Montalcino in Tuscany, known for being aged for over a decade in wood barrels. The wine was introduced on the international market the previous year. The Athenaeum, one of the premier London gentlemen's clubs, benefits from the fact that one of the members of The Society for Supernatural and Psychic Research that Scarlet and Pierce-Jones belong to is Enzo Conti, vintner and importer of renowned wines from Italy.

Magic Show.' But these two are different. They're not only both exceptional conjurers in performance. They both excel at creating extraordinary stage illusions. Actually, that's not a surprise where one of them is concerned."

"Who?"

"Giuseppe Caliosto—who bills himself as Marco the Magnificent. His father was a cabinet-maker, and taught his son the art. Did you know that most magicians come from a family background of either watchmaking or cabinet-making?"

"No, I didn't. But it makes perfect sense."

"Of course, it does," agreed Pierce-Jones. "Most of the big illusions in a magician's act depend upon mechanical design more than anything."

"Such as the disappearing cabinet?"

"Absolutely. Despite the name, it's the person inside who disappears, of course, not the cabinet.

"Incidentally," Django added, "there's your link to the spiritualists' acts you asked about. The spirit cabinet featured by the Americans the Davenport Brothers in the 1850s was a very famous conjuring act. The brothers were tied hand and foot and placed in a locked cabinet with an assortment of musical instruments. Once the cabinet door was closed and locked, music would begin to play, bells would ring, and so on, apparently all of it produced on those instruments.

"At some point in the midst of all this, the cabinet door would be unlocked and opened by an assistant. The brothers could be seen inside, still securely tied. Supposedly, spirits from the Great Beyond were producing the music. It was all part of the Spiritualism mania which gripped America, starting with the Fox Sisters' first public performance in 1849."

"And people believed in these invisible musicians?"

"Of course. They were Americans."

Pierce-Jones waited for Scarlet to finish laughing.

"Actually, it wasn't long before well-known magicians in

Europe and America started debunking the Davenports' act and demonstrating how the tricks were really accomplished. Your man Caliosto was one of the principal debunkers, by the way."

"But why would fellow conjurers reveal the secrets of magic illusions?"

"Ah—a very pretty question," replied Pierce-Jones. "Evidently, it's a point of honor for them. Professional magicians don't want people to think they possess supernatural abilities. You can see how easily that could be the case, since they seem to suspend or contradict natural laws, as if they had extraordinary powers. They openly admit that they are what they call honest conjurers, who perform illusions solely for entertainment. Only the dishonest and charlatans claim otherworldly powers."

"Catherine said the same thing," Scarlet admitted. "Apparently, people hold on to their illusions."

"Are you sure you don't mean delusions? Magicians are master psychologists, my friend."

Scarlet didn't want to go down that road at the moment.

"Does Caliosto—Marco the Magnificent—still make the exposure of spiritualism part of his act?" he asked.

"No, that's old hat now," replied Django. "The best stage acts are those that keep coming up with new illusions. Sometimes that means building on the tricks of rivals, or coming up with entirely new effects."

"And what is Marco the Magnificent known for now?"

"Well, he's accomplished at all of the major illusions that most of the masters perform these days. But he's best known for The Bullet Catch."

"What in the world is that?"

"It's just what it sounds like," replied Pierce-Jones. "A volunteer from the audience fires a rifle point-blank at the magician. Sometimes, it's a firing squad dressed in military uniforms. If it's one individual firing the weapon, he or she inspects and marks the round beforehand . . . they're always real bullets, incidentally. If it's a firing squad, the audience volunteer hands the bullets to the marksmen. It's apparently an article of faith among magicians that this audience volunteer is never a plant. The rifle or rifles are then fired at the magician from just a few feet away, and he catches the single bullet or all of them in one hand. Sometimes, he catches a single bullet in his teeth."

"What!"

"I'm not exaggerating, old boy. That's exactly the way it's done."

"Extraordinary," said Scarlet. "Is it considered dangerous?"

"As far as I can tell, it *is* dangerous," replied Django. "But defying death has always been part of the attraction of great magicians' shows."

"I should say," agreed Scarlet.

Dessert and coffee had come by then, and the two men attended to it, still considering, perhaps, the implications of The Bullet Catch. Finally, Scarlet asked:

"And what about Max von Leiden?"

"'The Master of Illusion,'" added Django. "He's an entirely different kettle of fish from Marco the Magnificent. To begin with, he's really German, not a made-up stage German. His stage act is called *Phantasmagoria*. Marco's, incidentally, is called *The Cabalistic Laboratory*."

"What's von Leiden's show like?"

"Much darker than Caliosto's. In fact, von Leiden has a much more mysterious persona. He looks the part, for one thing—he's tall, with dark hair and a peaked hairline, black moustaches and a goatee, and large, arching eyebrows. His fingers are extraordinarily long and delicate. He has a reputation for going beyond traditional magic, for pushing the boundaries of nature and manipulating human psychology."

"How does he do such a thing?"

"I honestly don't know, Will. You'll have to attend a show and report back."

"Indeed, I'll do that. What's he known for? Aside from playing the mysterious dark stranger, I mean?"

Django Pierce-Jones thought about his answer.

"It's an odd thing," he said. "He apparently grants people's wishes."

"You must be joking."

"I'm not. I really don't know much about it, but apparently it's true. The claim, I mean. I understand it's a special part of his act— one he performs only occasionally. I hear there's no knowing beforehand whether he will be performing it that night with a volunteer from the audience."

"All the more reason for people to flock to his shows, I would think," said Scarlet. "Not knowing whether this will be the night, I mean."

"It would certainly have that effect, wouldn't it?" said Django.

He looked at his friend closely.

"There's a spark in your eye, old man," he said, and quoted: "'I see you stand like greyhounds in the slips/Straining upon the start.'"

"Yes—the game's afoot," continued Scarlet, who knew his Shakespeare as well as Pierce-Jones.

GARY GENARD is the author of the Dr. William Scarlet mysteries. He lives in Massachusetts. You can find his fiction and nonfiction books at **www.garygenard.com**.

Printed in Great Britain
by Amazon

42442083R00128